HERB

AND THE MAGIC MILK TRUCK

Mark T. Holmes

Also by the author:

The Last Flight of Chauncey Freeman

Artifact – A Novel of World War II

Always Ready – Coast Guard Sea Stories From the 1970s

Streams to Ford

This is a work of fiction, not a factual account. Names, characters, businesses, places, events and incidents are either the products of the author's imagination or used in a fictitious manner. Any resemblance to actual persons, living or dead, or actual events is purely coincidental.

Acknowledgments

The author would like to specifically thank Mr. Ken Ballard, Sr., who provided highly detailed information about the life and the work of a milkman in the era of this story. In fact, Mr. Ballard was a milkman with 41 years of service to two Danbury area dairies, and his insight was indispensable in creating an authentic character.

Additional very helpful resources included:

Sheila Hislop
Steven Holmes
Bonnie Gallo Johnson
Tracey Pevehouse
Don Preiser
Lyneen Smith
Michael C. Wilson
ConnecticutHistory.org
CTVISIT.com
Google Maps
Wikipedia

Prologue

When I was growing up in the 1950s and 1960s, it was common in my hometown of Danbury, Connecticut, to see all types of services delivered directly to our home and to thousands of others. Among them was the milkman in his little delivery truck along with a lady who delivered eggs, the insurance man who would come by the house to collect the five-dollar premium every month, the Charles Chips delivery guy, oil delivery trucks, and even our family doctor.

This story is about fictional milkman Herb Lundy and his encounter with a spiritual being that provides him with the opportunity to take a journey through time and faith. The story is interjected with the observations of the author growing up in the same town roughly at the same time, reflecting on a lifestyle in the late 1950s that is long gone but fondly remembered.

Don't forget, this is a work of fiction. There is no Magic Dairy, nor is it supposed to represent Marcus Dairy. Danburians, in particular, will remember a lot of details, may dispute some, and will have to understand that this is a mixture of fact, fiction, and my own imagination. Enjoy.

Chapter One

It was a gorgeous, mid-April morning in Danbury, Connecticut, the type of day that made children yearn for the end of the school year and parents dream of upcoming summer vacations along the rugged coast of Maine, at a lakeside cabin in New Hampshire, or maybe a cottage on the Cape. The last of the rock-hard ice that lined the curbs of most streets was nearly gone, the melting snow creating tiny streams that ran down Seeley Street, Deer Hill Avenue, Town Hill Avenue, and all the other rolling streets that were carefully laid out across the historic Western New England town.

At the corner of Deer Hill Avenue and West Street, the First Congregational Church rose impressively to the blue sky above, the gold cupola topped by a tall weathervane that capped the space over a massive bell enclosure. Beneath that, still on the tower, four large clock faces showed the time in each direction, so there could be no doubt. All of this sat on a meticulously maintained brick and stone building. Founded in 1696, the congregation was one of the oldest in the nation, and the church with its tall Grecian columns was massive and intimidating to a young boy like me.

My sister and I attended Sunday school somewhere in a classroom deep inside the wood-lined interior of the church auxiliary spaces while my parents sat in a middle-aisle spot in a pew about half-way between the huge pipe organ, raised pulpit, and choir stand, and the massive front doors. To my father, it seemed like a safe place – not too close to the sermon, not too far from the exit. In this way, he did not fully commit one way or the other but hedged his bets with weekly attendance.

Much closer to the front of the sanctuary, where the giant pipe organ thundered with the music of the "three B's," Bach, Brahms, and Beethoven, the organist's hands flailed about wildly, under the careful eye of Herb Lundy, one of the local milkmen who delivered for Magic Dairy. Herb felt lucky that his delivery schedule allowed him Sunday as a day off; some other drivers were not so lucky. In fact, Sunday was Herb's *only* day off and he enjoyed it thoroughly.

Back in 1957, every job it seemed, offered a respectful wage, one that allowed a man to feed his family and afford a modest home and decent car. Those who worked harder and smarter could afford a little more. It was all anyone needed, and it was all most people wanted.

The more entrepreneurial few, those with larger homes on impressive lots owned the businesses that lined Main Street or operated oil delivery and commodity distributors and held sway at city hall, a low brick building cut into the ground across the street from the church.

The owner of Magic Dairy was one such man, and he resided in a modern Frank Lloyd Wright-looking home set back from the street on lower Deer Hill Avenue.

Frank Mark, the man with two first names, hired only the best people and paid them more than fairly, and as a result, the loyalty of his employees fed through to his customers who avoided buying milk in those new cartons from the Grand Union or the A&P but preferred instead to keep receiving regular deliveries of milk bottles at their front door steps brought by the drivers from Magic Dairy.

As church let out in time for moms to finish making the obligatory early afternoon "dinner," churchgoers idled out on the white stone steps, chatting with the minister and shaking hands with people they knew or simply nodding to strangers who caught their eye. Someone approached the mayor and whispered something in his ear. Both men laughed. Women donned jackets and children jumped and bounced, having been let out of Sunday school lessons in time to join their parents in the main sanctuary and hear the familiar, comforting benediction by Reverend Waller and the choir's closing hymn:

> *Praise God from whom all blessings flow;*
> *Praise Him all creatures here below;*
> *Praise Him above, ye heavenly host;*
> *Praise Father, Son, and Holy Ghost.*
> *Amen.*

The song lingered in my head for an hour or two every Sunday afternoon. It resonated more deeply though, with Herb.

Herb Lundy lingered out front longer than most, intrigued by the sermon he'd witnessed, close enough to the elevated pulpit to see up the minister's nose, truth be told. He liked having that up close and personal connection, even if he didn't know why. Being that close to the holy words brought a bit of comfort but it all seemed so vast and mysterious despite the reverend's attempts to put God's teachings into contemporary terms.

Herb often fretted about not being a complete Christian. He thought he was missing something. He prayed on a regular basis and gave thanks for his many blessings. He asked God to look over his family and to extend His Grace to those in need. He tried but had never read the entire Bible. He'd read the New Testament often, over in England, on board his airplane flying back from bombing missions, and sometimes at home. He tried to help the poor when he could. But still, when it came to his faith, he felt like a 100-piece puzzle with a few pieces missing. It made him uneasy.

Because of a doting older sister, Herb began school with a leg up on everyone else. His sister Marcy spent hours with him teaching him what she knew. Four years older than Herb, she was already in fifth grade when Herb was enrolled in the first grade. Marcy's tutoring when he was just a toddler had a profound effect on Herb's ability to assimilate information. He sponged up the lessons and once shown a method or concept, could master it. He wasn't quite bored with school, but the work came easily, and Herb sported a string of "A's" on his report cards with no more effort than a sous chef cooking a custard dessert. Learning stayed that way until high school came, and he met the evil twins; calculus and trigonometry.

Until that fateful year, Herb breezed through school, homework done in a flash. Concepts once represented were easily understood, but not calculus and not trig. The teacher didn't explain the why and how of it; he simply dove into the book, as if the students already knew the material. Other students seemed to grasp the advanced math, but despite his ease in absorbing algebra and geometry, these horrible areas of study were and remained completely foreign to Herb. With that mathematical roadblock, Herb began to question his own worth. He didn't know how to attack a problem that made no sense. He didn't know how to do the work. The gift his sister gave no longer functioned. Something was wrong.

At the same time, Herb mostly quit going to church. It was the same thing every week; a couple of songs poorly sung by the parishioners, a sermon he'd heard several times over, the passing of the offering plate while adults idly gossiped about who was wearing what. It was enough. With schoolwork becoming increasingly difficult after a lifetime of ease and the lack of churchly influence, Herb was lost. Worse yet, war was upon the country. The men of Danbury began to disappear to the draft board or volunteered outright. Before long, he would be of age and among them. His carefully forged and easily poured foundation was crumbling underneath him and Herb for the first time, felt hopelessly and horribly clueless.

The months flew by and before long, Herb was on a train to Texas to learn aerial gunnery before heading off to the European Theatre. At first, he learned to fire a machine gun from the back of a moving truck, then it was on to aerial gunnery, learning all the tips and tricks he could to help him survive the ordeal ahead. Before long, Herb joined up with his B-24 bomber crew and they began formal training with the rest of the newly created 392nd Bomb Group. Within a few months, they were on their way to Wendling, England to join the war. Herb took the small New Testament Bible his mother had given to him as an insurance policy, and something to read on long trips back to England from bombing runs over France and Germany. He didn't know if what he was reading was true, but he also didn't want to tempt the fates just in case. They say being in battle will make you a believer. Herb never had that revelation even during a flak barrage or the bullets and cannon fire from oncoming Focke-Wulf and Messerschmidt fighters. It just wasn't in him. Try as he might, what he felt most was emptiness. Herb wasn't sad, nor was he necessarily fearful, just empty.

While grateful for returning from the war mostly unscathed, Herb's uncertainty surrounding his faith clung to him no matter how hard he tried to work it out from the first pew of the First Congregational Church.

"Reverend Waller." Herb nodded while he stuck his hand out towards the bulky minister with the big smile, fiery red hair, and nearly redder complexion. He grabbed and encased the smaller man's hand with gusto.

"Yes, hello Mr. Lundy. So good to see you again in the front row. Most people are shy about sitting up there for some reason."

"Well, I like to be close to whatever it is I'm doing. I also really like the sound from the pipe organ in that spot."

"The sound does fill the sanctuary but yes, there are several places where it's particularly clear, like up near the pulpit. People don't know what they're missing."

Small talk aside, Herb Lundy wanted to be near the reverend; to be in the presence of one who communed with the Lord, or so it would seem. He didn't know why, nor could he explain it to June, his wife, who pulled on Herb's coat. Her roast beef needed to come out of the oven soon. Timing was everything, and by starting the roast before they left for church, it would be just medium-rare by the time they got home. Herb waved goodbye to the reverend and shook a few more hands on the way to the parking lot. So many friends; so many good customers.

Chapter Two

Like every morning, Monday through Saturday, Herb Lundy rolled out of his twin bed, feet finding his slippers automatically through years of practice. Dawn would not grace the cold morning sky for quite some time yet, but he needed to get to work and prepare his milk run for the day. Herb found the early morning hour to be especially peaceful, allowing him a few moments to leisurely enjoy a cup of coffee and think about today's route.

Every Monday and Thursday, Herb's milk run covered the south side of Danbury including the area around Rogers Park and over to nearby Bethel. It was his longest of the three routes he served, covering dozens of miles and serving more than a hundred homes, small stores, and schools. Herb enjoyed the chance to pass through Rogers Park twice a week, stopping briefly to admire the rose trellises and lingering along the shady avenue before having his lunch, then finishing up his daily run along Mountainville Road, back up Southern Boulevard and across Deer Hill Avenue before heading down steep Seeley Street and back across Rogers Park to the Coalpit Road neighborhoods.

Rogers Park originated years earlier when

the initial plot was donated by local industrialist Cephas Rogers who agreed to donate twenty acres of swampy land near the corner of South Street and Main Street in exchange for forgiveness of a $6,000 tax debt resulting from hard times in the 1930s. Cephas and the town council members cut the ribbon to the park in 1941 and as years passed, the city annexed surrounding land until it grew to more than fifty acres. Herb enjoyed driving through the park connecting one milk route to another and frequently stopped under a big elm tree near the pond to eat his sandwich for lunch.

The pond served as a fishing hole for youngsters such as me, and we caught undersized bream, sunfish and the occasional perch if we were lucky. Hours were spent in the summer sun watching our red and white bobbers, waiting for the next big strike. Occasionally during our outings in the summer, we'd notice a Magic Dairy truck parked under the big tree, the slender and serene-looking driver stopping to have his lunch.

In the winter, the pond made an ideal skating rink complete with a shore-side warm-up hut that hosted a toasty fire in a cast-iron stove and a huge loudspeaker that played the top-40 hit songs. Next to the pond was a large playing field where Sunday soccer matches were played by Hispanic players who shouted, "Aqui, aqui!" as they ran to and fro, playing a game I did not understand nor appreciate. In between the pond and the soccer field, the stately elm tree cast shade for hot summer days or afforded some privacy for a parked car with two lovers inside.

Today, however, the tree would serve a vastly different purpose. A fellow survivor of the Dutch elm disease that robbed Danbury of many of its stately elms, it was not as impressive as the three-hundred-year-old Garfield Elm located across town, but its newly budded leaves shimmered brightly like shiny garland in the crisp morning breeze, as if the entire tree somehow knew today would be different from all other days.

Herb Lundy took every aspect of his work seriously; a lesson learned a dozen years ago standing at his gunner's station in the fuselage of a lumbering B-24 Liberator. The heavy bomber was a reliable conveyance and an assortment of them ferried Herb and his fellow crewmembers across the English Channel and back home no less than thirty-five times. In the skies over Germany, where the air at altitude was so cold that it hurt, Herb gained the ability to focus keenly on any task at hand, mostly the two or three seconds of terror when a German ME-109 or Focke-Wulf 190 came screaming towards his plane, the pilot intent on destroying him.

Over the course of six months, Herb

recorded several kills and as one mission piled on top of the previous, he fine-tuned his ability to anticipate the moves of his adversary, leading with his .50-caliber Browning machine gun perfectly, chewing up the wings and cockpit of increasingly desperate Luftwaffe pilots and their rapidly disappearing planes.

What shook him to the core however was the flak; "fliegerabwehrkanone" was the actual German word, but the abbreviation, "flak" was all that was needed to convey the terror. Huge multi-story concrete flak towers constructed in strategic locations below and flak "boxes" of grid-like concentrated 88mm guns filled the skies with red-hot metal shards as the 8th Air Force bombers approached hardened targets like Cologne or areas west of Berlin. From his gunner's window, Herb saw planes filled with friends and brothers-in-arms explode or fall helplessly from the sky. He dared not think if his plane was next.

Casually noting the model B-24 he had carved from mahogany years ago sitting atop the glassed-in walnut hallway cabinet, Herb grabbed his Magic Dairy jacket and hat, shuddered at the memories and headed outside, his dog-eared paperback copy of H.G. Wells' *The Time Machine* tucked under his arm. Although he'd read it twice before, the story made for a good diversion during his lunch break under the elm tree in

Rogers Park. It was still dark outside, but the forty-two-degree air and sharp breeze brought Herb fully awake as he settled behind the wheel of his maroon '54 Ford sedan, shifted into gear and headed over to the Magic Dairy farm.

Like other local dairies, Magic brought in raw milk from nearby and distant farms, processed, pasteurized and bottled it, offering home delivery to Danbury and surrounding areas. Men like Herb Lundy kept the dairy profitable through efficient and reliable delivery, selling additional products and tracking down overdue payments. Experience counted and so did a positive personality.

Chapter Three

Herb knew his daily routes better than he knew the alphabet, and to amuse himself, he timed the routes almost every day, setting a record for each route and attempting to beat it. It was personally important that his customers could rely on him to serve them at the appointed time and measuring each day's run was a way to gauge his own success in this somewhat self-centered endeavor. Besides, happy customers were more eager to buy additional products – cream, eggnog during the holidays, cottage cheese, sour cream, and even eggs. He knew enough though, not to compete with Edna the egg lady and if one of his customers got eggs from Edna, he'd sell them something else rather than steal business from her even though she could not retaliate. It was a small point of honor but for Herb and men like him, it may as well have been a commandment.

Each daily record was in fact, two records; one before lunch and one after. The faster he completed his morning run, the more time he entitled himself to lunch – sometimes. After all, he was not on the clock; when his deliveries were complete, the remaining ice flushed out of his truck and other menial chores complete, the rest of the day belonged to him.

The south route was Herb's most challenging of the three, meandering over the hilly landscape of western and southwestern Danbury and over to nearby Bethel with many houses, mainly along Deer Hill Avenue, set well back from the street, resulting in extra time to drop off the milk bottles and collect the empties.

Navigating the steep hills during the latter part of his run was a nearly joyless task; the humble little 4-cylinder Divco delivery truck was reliable but severely underpowered. Heading up Southern Boulevard off Mountainville Road, then ascending Deer Hill Avenue was a challenge made slightly easier by the fact the truck was lighter now than earlier in the day, but driving gingerly down Seeley Street was always a thrill, the rather timid brakes squeaking and squealing against relentless gravity to loudly announce his arrival at each home along the way.

In the winter, the low gearing of the Divco truck made it easier for Herb and other drivers to navigate through the snow and icy roads. Chains helped and some days, it was nearly impossible to get through, but like the other drivers, Herb persevered; after all, no sales, no commission.

Herb knew almost all his customers by name and in most cases, he simply walked into the home and put the milk directly into the refrigerator, collecting the empties on his way out. If someone was home, he'd ask if they wanted something else from the truck and if so, he'd go get it, adding to his commission. If no one was home, he'd often leave a flyer showing the current special offers. Like the other drivers, Herb was responsible for sales, billing, and collection and he got paid a bonus to collect overdue payments along with his extra commission for selling additional products. By being friendly and persistent, Herb made enough income to avoid taking a second job in the afternoon as some other drivers were compelled to do. With half an afternoon free most days, Herb felt like a king and why not?

On the chilly but sun-filled April day, Herb would need that extra time in the afternoon to consider the inconceivable miracle that was about to happen.

Chapter Four

Stan Solomon owned and operated the Main Street Bake Shop, a store he'd taken over from his father Simon, back in 1946. Although the wonderful aromas of baking bread were lost on Stan, having been involved with the store as a boy, and then again after the war, his customers couldn't wait for their special day to come in for a dozen hard rolls, a birthday cake, French bread, or any of the other freshly-made products that filled the glass cases in the busy store.

For Herb Lundy, his day to visit the Main Street Bake Shop was Sunday, right after church, like many other Danburians. Herb got extra special treatment, with his order ready to go and a running tab so he didn't have to wait at the checkout counter. He also got a hearty wave and hello from Stan, his boyhood friend and to this day, his best friend.

Nearly every Sunday, we would run into Mr. Lundy at the shop, not by random coincidence, but because it was our family's tradition to stop in after church, too. When my dad didn't feel like getting out of the car, which was often, he'd send my sister and me in to buy our dozen hard rolls, which Stan always insisted equaled thirteen rolls instead of twelve. He called it a "baker's dozen" and although a small touch, it made us feel just a little special.

Almost every Sunday while waiting in line to place our order, we'd see the man who sat up front in church breeze in and out, waving to Mr. Solomon and walking out without paying. How did he do that? We thought he must have been a family member.

Like many Danbury families, our Sunday "dinner" was the big meal of the day at around two o'clock when my mother would present a pork roast, roast beef, or maybe a turkey breast along with potatoes, carrots, and a bowl of peas or green beans. The leftover meat was carefully sliced and served on Main Street Bake Shop hard rolls with a big pot of tea for supper later. The tea may have been more of a tradition carried over by my grandma, a native of Norwich in the East Anglia section of England. This light supper was not a sometimes event; it was a Sunday ritual and became one of our little treasures to look forward to each week, sitting in the living room with our food perched on folding metal tray tables eating slowly while waiting for the Ed Sullivan Show to come on.

At the Lundy home, June followed the same routine although with Herb's early morning schedule, pushed back the "dinner" hour to three o'clock and it served as their supper as well, with just a light snack later since Herb turned in by nine in order to get up at the unholy hour of 4 a.m. to make it to the dairy one hour later to begin loading his truck.

The workers at the dairy had it harder, working overnight to prepare the outbound loads of milk, cream, and the other dairy products, and starting to load cheesecloth bags full of ice used to cover the perishable milk bottles as the drivers made their rounds during the day. Each driver would augment their loads with products that were on special that week or those they knew they could easily sell to eager customers.

To a novice, it would seem impossible to know what to load and how much, but most drivers at Magic Dairy were veterans of many years of service and could predict their sales almost to the dollar. Herb was one of them and one of the best to be quite honest. He seldom returned his truck with anything but empty bottles and dripping cheesecloth bags. Skills and results such as these made Frank Mark smile and made him a happy and wealthy man.

Chapter Five

Danbury Connecticut was an old New England town, named after Danbury, Essex in England; a village some thirty miles northeast of London and the place where many area settlers had originated. After being known as Swampfield for the first couple of years, our Danbury was first named way back in 1687, nine years before the church that became my First Congregational Church was formed. Danbury was officially incorporated in 1702 and then chartered as a city much later, in 1889. The town served as a supply depot for the Revolutionary Army and in fact, was raided and burned by British troops led by General William Tryon in April of 1777.

Generals' names from the war were attached to places we frequented: (General Israel – "Old Put") Putnam Park, plus (General David) Wooster Street, Wooster School, and the undulating and serene Wooster Cemetery near Danbury Hospital. History was everywhere: even the weathered old Keeler Tavern in nearby Ridgefield still held a cannonball lodged into the side of the building from the 1777 skirmish with the British.

Through much of the nineteenth century

and to the 1920s, Danbury was regarded as the hat city of the world, and hats continued to be a major industry well into the twentieth century. In the late 1800s, no less than thirty hat factories spewed out one and a half million hats a year but by end of World War II, the industry had quickly faded, as hat-wearing trends came to an end, and as a young child, I knew of only one remaining factory, Stetson, still producing hats. The empty factories fell into disrepair and were demolished to use the spaces for other purposes. Every Danbury child knew its history, but it all seemed like a faint and only mildly interesting shadow.

Nonetheless, the Danbury High School mascot name was "Hatters" and the name even survived a vote by the student body to change it to something more relevant in the mid-1960s. Some traditions were too well steeped to discard.

Danbury shrugged off winter like a young socialite un-shouldering her cape at the cloakroom of a ritzy New York nightclub, eager to enjoy whatever came next. The pent-up energy of thirty-five thousand or so men, women, and children was palpable and probably enough, if captured, to light up the city for the entire summer. Jackets were cleaned and put away for the next five months. Smudge pots marked off sections of roadway where city crews busily repaired the worst of the potholes. Danbury High School baseball was in full swing as April gave way to May, with local legend Clayton Haviland taking over as coach, and kids like us swept their backyards with flashlights and tin cans, collecting nightcrawlers for the next day's fishing adventure.

Our Sunday drives around western and northwestern Connecticut now included the distinctive voices and announcing styles of Mel Allen and Red Barber as they called Yankee games on the radio. Several times a season, our dad would treat us with a trip to the Bronx and Yankee Stadium. He would favor the aisle seat making it easier to catch the attention of the Ballantine Ale vendor who opened a can with four lightning-swift piercings with the can opener, pouring a torrent of brew from the gaping hole into a wax-lined paper cup as he looked up for his next customer.

At a game versus the Detroit Tigers, the whole family sat together in the upper deck on the third-base side. A foul ball was struck, heading directly for my mother's face as she sat there unaware. In one smooth move, I watched in awe as my dad switched his beer cup from his right hand to his left, and casually made a backhand catch of the ball, two inches away from my mom's nose without spilling a drop of his Ballantine. The adjacent crowd went wild as my dad held up his prize, handing it to me when the cheering stopped.

Going to Yankees games with my dad was the closest we ever really got. He was emotionally shut down from his experiences in World War II and while he never struck any of us kids, he was the subject of his own father's wrath and lash growing up. Still, nothing could beat an afternoon at Yankee stadium with your dad.

Herb Lundy and his best friend Stan tried to attend Sunday games when they could, but with the bake shop's schedule, it was a rare occasion when the two could escape for a game. When they did, they bought seats behind the screen near home plate, maybe twenty rows up, spending the extra few dollars for an up-close experience since their visits were so rare. The crusty old red-hatted ushers would guide them to their seats, half-heartedly dusting the chairs with an old rag, attempting to be useful, scavenging for a tip.

On other afternoons after his delivery route was finished, Herb would grab his new little Sony TR-63 transistor radio and a couple of Rheingold or Narragansett beers and head over to his father's place in Newtown to catch the rest of a day game on the radio. He'd bring peanuts or Cracker Jack too, and they'd sit next to each other, as fans in the stands, eyes fixed on some distant, imaginary point while Mel and Red described the action to perfection with their complementary and polite southern accents.

Between innings, commercials ran for Chock Full O' Nuts, the heavenly coffee, Castro Convertible furniture, the conqueror of living space, and ads that encouraged listeners to see the USA in your Chevrolet.

Spring meant switching from winter coats to lightweight jackets, pumping air into bicycle tires, and for several of the boys in my neighborhood, the start of fishing season. Oh, we tried ice fishing a few times on Candlewood Lake, but it all seemed like a lot of effort for little reward. The only thing I remember about ice fishing there was frozen fingers and sleek iceboats racing across the far side of the lake.

Fishing was just as important to us as baseball and we did both religiously and relentlessly. Come May, school was little more than an interruption to our fishing and baseball games and on a cool spring day, it was not uncommon to run home from South Street School, gather up either fishing gear or ball, bat, and glove and head to Rogers Park. This day, there was an early release for some reason no student cared about; all we knew is that we were told to go home early. No problem.

Rather than take the long and tedious route around to the entrance of the park off South Street near the Rogers Park Pharmacy, we'd typically just cut through Mr. Visconti's driveway on Mountainville Road because the back of his house faced the first ball field and he was not usually around to yell at us for doing so. That April day, however, was our first day for fishing, and while our bikes transported us all over town, to more far-flung spots like West Lake Reservoir or Tarrywile Lake, or even Candlewood Lake, way across town, a visit to the pond at Rogers Park was easily achievable on the shortened school day. And so, we went, racing through the park, fishing pole tucked into one hand holding a bike grip and the handle of the tackle box held in the other.

Rolling up to the pond that day, it became obvious that something was out of place. Or rather, something was there that should not have been there; namely, a milk truck from Magic Dairy. It was not unusual during the summer to see one of the trucks parked under the huge elm tree before noon, its driver munching a sandwich during a quick break, but at twelve-thirty in the afternoon, it made no sense. Even kids knew these trucks were usually finishing up their routes by then, or shortly after. Adding to the mystery, inside the new-looking truck the driver did not seem to be in a hurry, nor was he eating lunch. He was just sitting there reading a book.

Shrugging it off, we kids turned to our task at hand, or more accurately, the joy at hand, because fishing was about the best activity kids like us could do, so we eagerly baited hooks and checked the red and white bobbers, and for reasons unknown, attempted to cast our lines as far into the water as possible, as if the bigger fish would be waiting there, and there alone.

A small plane flew overhead, the distant drone of the engine cutting through the blue sky. Birds chirped and flew from tree to limb. The occasional car drove by and the sound of workers building a trampoline park nearby could be heard across the breeze. The occasional swear words caught our ears and we carefully stored those words away for future reference.

My friend Randy had a new open-face spinning reel of which I was insanely jealous, for my bait-casting reel frequently seized up in a rat's nest of jumbled fishing line every time I did not catch the spool with my thumb just right as the line hit the water. Any extra spinning of the spool made for five minutes of fevered untangling, hoping to the Lord that I did not get a bite while sorting out the line and softly repeating some of the words I'd heard from the nearby workers.

After a while, with no fish on the line so far, a breeze kicked up and then got stronger. And stronger. We looked around. No clouds. No obvious reason for a breeze to appear so suddenly, and yet it was there, blowing debris across the nearby roadway, kicking up ripples on the pond. As soon as it had started, it abruptly stopped. What was it? A zephyr? Randy and I looked quizzically at each other and then for some reason, we looked over at the Magic Dairy truck, now flanked by a dazed and confused looking driver. He was not alone. And then suddenly, he was.

Chapter Six

Growing up in the center of a town with a rich history, and more attuned to it as children in the 1920s on into the Depression, Herb Lundy and Stan Solomon actually loved the old artifacts and stories that living in Danbury presented. Before opening the Main Street Bake Shop, Stan's father Simon worked at the Lowery Hat Company, a smaller shop located in a two-story wooden building along the Still River off Triangle Street. In the '20s, hat factories began to close due to a decline in demand, and Lowery was one of the first to go. Seeing no future in the hat industry, Simon turned his baking hobby into a business and with most of his meager funds removed from the Union Savings Bank along with a handshake loan from a young entrepreneur named Jacob Mark, the Main Street Bake Shop was born.

Stan and Herb lived in separate apartments in a three-story house on Wildman Street, near enough to the Lowery Hat Company for Stan's father to walk to work, and close enough so that the boys could hear the trains arriving and leaving the nearby Danbury train station off White Street. The Solomon family lived on the second floor and the Lundy family occupied the third floor while the owners made their home on the ground floor. The Solomon family knew when the Lundy family was moving about on the floor above, and in spite of Mr. Solomon's attempts to quietly shuffle around the apartment as he prepared to leave for work, Mrs. Winston, the homeowner on the first floor always knew when her tenant left for the day. The gray and white home featured a large, wrap-around porch where the adults would sit, smoke, and chat on summer evenings while the boys chased and caught fireflies in the nearby fields or had a catch before it became too dark.

It was less than a mile's walk to reach the new bake shop on Main Street so Mr. Solomon typically walked to work, even in the harshest snowstorm or rainy April mornings to begin baking for the day, winding his way past Chestnut Street, across Liberty Street and finally connecting to Main Street by the short Keeler Street. The walk invigorated him and gave him time to clear his head from the painfully early alarm clock, letting him plan his day.

Occasionally, he'd meet a man waiting by the back door of his shop looking for a handout of yesterday's bread. Sometimes he'd find a young woman there, too. They weren't there every morning, and they weren't always the same folks. Word got out that a good man on Main Street would give you bread, rolls, or even cookies if you asked politely.

Some of Simon's contemporaries called these people bums. He called them human beings and gladly handed over the day-old baked goods he could no longer sell, refusing the offer of payment. No one knew about it until years later when Simon fell ill and more than a few strangers visited him at Danbury Hospital in his final days; strangers he had helped and who had moved on to better days. Young Stanley Solomon absorbed in wonder, the outpouring of affection from people he'd never met as his dad passed in late 1946 and took a lesson he'd never forget.

Several blocks down from the boys' apartment building there was a train whistle crossing where Wildman Street met Triangle Street, and as trains arrived from Bethel, reaching the last stop on the line in Danbury, the train horns, chugging engines, and clanging warning bells became part of the symphony of the boys' neighborhood. Who or what was on those trains? Were there wealthy businessmen from New York City? A carload of exotic fruit from some foreign island? Stan and Herb made a game where they guessed the cargo and though the contents were never proved, the game fed their imaginations and made them dream of travel to distant places, and for Herb, distant times.

Chapter Seven

Herb pulled into the employee lot at Magic Dairy out on Miry Brook Road, near the municipal airport and not far from the popular Danbury State Fair. He parked in his usual space closest to the gate. The gravel parking lot gave off a crunchy sound under his work boots and hints of an overnight frost could be found on the metal railing and along the edge of the door marked, "Drivers Only."

Since each in the fleet of delivery trucks routinely accumulated many hundreds of miles per month, frequent maintenance was called for and sometimes, the drivers would be assigned to one truck or another. It made no difference, as the Divco trucks were essentially identical but most drivers ended up with a regular ride. The Detroit Industrial Vehicles Company trucks were designed for the purpose; all-steel construction and an eager if somewhat milquetoast 4-cylinder motor under the sloped hood. Inside, the truck was no-nonsense, built to haul milk, a driver, and if available an assistant. The driver could sit if he wanted, but getting up and down a hundred times a day could be tedious and so the little Divco had controls on the steering column that allowed the driver to stand and drive, making it easier to hop out and back in the truck at each stop along the way. The only real safety shortcoming was that the clutch and brake shared a pedal in an odd design, making a sudden, unintended stop a real possibility for a less than careful driver. Herb preferred to stand, and he also preferred to work alone so even in the summer when part-time runners were available, he kept to himself instead of having to entertain a chatty and absent-minded high school kid.

Herb's regular truck was in for brake service and a clutch swap, so he was assigned a brand new, just delivered Divco truck, complete with a fresh paint job and the red and blue Magic Dairy logo made to look like a rabbit and top hat. Each truck sported a small painted American flag on each side of the hood, faintly resembling mounted flags flying on a general's jeep.

Like so many others, Magic Dairy owner Frank Mark had proudly served in the war and in fact, so did most of his drivers. The placement of the flags on each Magic Dairy truck was no symbol of casual patriotism; it was a testament to God and the American Way, and every driver knew it.

Harry "Bucko" Stevens worked the loading dock with an energy that nearly defied description. A former lineman for the Danbury High School Hatters football team, Harry earned all-state honors in 1951 earning the nickname

Bucko because for some reason that's the word he yelled every time the team made a big play. Following a short stint in the U.S. Army (he was discharged when a disk injury was identified in his back) he took on the job as loading dock assistant, earning a promotion within a year based on his eager approach to ... everything. From his early morning, ear-to-ear smile to the machine-like packing of ice bags, he was a non-stop dervish. The disk the Army had so worried about never affected his work. Harry made every driver's job easier and every driver showed their appreciation in kind with an envelope at the end of each month.

Loading up Herb's truck took less time than usual as Harry chatted non-stop about his beloved New York Yankees and the promise of the 1957 season. Herb Lundy started his route that fine April morning a full ten minutes early. Good. He might make the entire route without stopping for lunch until he was done. In fact, his big customer, South Street School was closing early, and he'd save a good eight minutes by skipping the elementary school with the long driveway and chatty kitchen staff.

Thinking ahead, Herb decided to make the run out to Coalpit Hill Road and the nursing home in Bethel that was normally the last of his route, swapping it for the run through Mountainville Road and Deer Hill Avenue.

Perhaps with a brand-new truck at his command, he'd even break his current record for the south side run: five hours and forty-eight minutes. Then, he'd reward himself with a leisurely lunch under the elm tree near the pond in Rogers Park. Maybe he'd even have time to finish *The Time Machine* before heading back to the dairy.

Chapter Eight

The new Divco milk truck drove like a dream compared to the two-year-old model Herb Lundy was accustomed to driving. Near-zero miles compared to fifty thousand miles was no comparison at all. The clutch was smooth as Rogers Park pond ice in January. The brakes did not grab or squeal and the little 4-banger seemed to have noticeably more power than the other trucks in the fleet. Herb breezed through his route and even managed to sell his predicted extra load of chocolate milk and heavy cream to eager housewives. Most of the seniors at the retirement home in Bethel were enjoying morning naps and thereby did not get to chat with their favorite visitor this day.

Herb cut through Rogers Park by the tennis courts and shallow cement pool and playground just off Coalpit Hill Road, took a right on Memorial Drive and turned left at the light on South Street. Five hundred feet later, he deftly turned his new truck onto Mountainville Road after stopping at two adjacent homes on South Street next to the small Studebaker dealership. In fact, it wasn't exactly a dealership if you think of big windows, shiny cars, and pushy salesmen; it was a small, brick-front garage with a few cars out front. I walked past it every day on my way to school and in the early sixties, marveled at the sleek Avanti out front.

Up-shifting like Pat Flaherty at the Brickyard, Herb whizzed past the bottom of Seeley Street and made his first stop on Mountainville Road, leaping to the task leaving full milk bottles and carting out empties. Herb was in a zone and time seemed to stand still as he sailed from one home to the next, like the bombardier on his old B-24 engaging autopilot at the initial point on a bomb run over Germany. As his mind wandered, Herb's "bombsight" was on the next home up ahead, and the milk bombs in his truck always hit their targeted refrigerators.

Herb did not think about the war very often and talked about it even less. The terrors were not forgotten but they were assuaged with the occasional highball at the VFW and in the loving arms of his patient wife, June. His ears rang constantly, a full-time reminder of the chattering Browning machine gun under his thumb for those six months of combat and the training before, in Texas. It was a small trade-off for the blessing of coming home alive when so many others in the 8th Air Force did not. Having stepped away from church late in high school, Herb somewhat tentatively rediscovered his faith in the belly of a B-24 and carried the small New Testament his mother gave him into battle, a diminutive leather-bound zippered book that revealed and assured his salvation on trips to Germany and back. It couldn't hurt, and it might just help.

Steering up Deer Hill Avenue past the stately homes, Herb snapped back to real time, taking on the slightly more tedious deliveries owing to some of the homes being set back from the street. No matter. The housewives and maids who worked in many of the homes frequently bought extras – cottage cheese, cream, and quarts of eggnog at Christmastime, making Herb additional money for doing little more work. It was a sweet deal and he smiled extra-wide to each customer, making suggestions for other products in a casual but firm way.

"You know, I've been selling a lot of fresh eggs lately. There seems to be a run on them for some reason." Herb was careful to avoid any of Edna's customers.

"Oh, really?" Spurred by this "news," many a housewife elected to schedule a dozen eggs for Herb's next visit three days hence. He once intruded into Edna the Egg Lady's territory with this sales pitch and feeling guilty, apologized profusely to the woman, promising to never let it happen again, and making up for it with a free bottle of heavy cream.

Herb eventually made a U-turn in the parking lot of city hall, across from the First

Congregational Church and headed back across Deer Hill Avenue stopping along the way before heading down steep Seeley Street (with his new-truck brakes) before crossing Housman Street all the way over to Southern Boulevard and retracing his route down Mountainville Road back to Rogers Park. He nearly sold out his truck, made some notes for future orders, and marked the time. If he held off on the sales pitch along the last section of his route, he'd be able to break his old record by five full minutes, he figured. With the robust sales Herb achieved on Deer Hill Avenue, he elected to hit-and-run on the remaining stops unless someone had a specific request. Herb arrived under the elm tree near the pond in Rogers Park at 11:42 a.m., setting a record for the south side route by three minutes. It was good enough.

The Divco truck chugged to a stop and finally, Herb sat down, reaching for his lunch pail. The temperature had warmed a bit, to the mid '60s and a very slight breeze wafted through the open truck doors. The only sounds were of unseen men troweling cement blocks over at the trampoline park under construction. Two boys fussed with tackle boxes near the pond.

Herb Lundy patiently downed his roast beef sandwich on a hard roll that was just slightly harder than yesterday, when he bought it. Still, it was an excellent sandwich, washed down with a pint of cold milk. The pickle June packed for him the night before, he would enjoy on the drive back to Magic Dairy. Settling into the last few chapters of his book, Herb did not look up when the breeze intensified. Not until his truck shook slightly in the now-stiff wind, did he really notice it. There were no clouds in the sky. What could it be? A temperature inversion of some sort?

He stepped down from the truck to check the sky when an odd voice called his name.

"Herb. HERB! Over here!"

Herb looked around but did not see anyone. The voice called out again.

"No, over here!" And then someone appeared next to Herb. Speaking more softly, "Here, Herb. Over here."

Herb shuddered and stepped back. The visage before him was a man, but not a man at the same time. His frame was a full three inches shorter than Herb's six-foot height, and the man's hair was uncharacteristically long, falling on his shoulders. He had a gentle appearance and offered a calming smile but did not seem either young nor old. His forehead showed evidence of a succession of small scars.

"I can't help but notice the book you're reading," said the stranger. "How would you like to try some time travel for yourself?"

Chapter Nine

Instinctively, Herb reached into the truck for the Louisville Slugger 34-ounce baseball bat he carried just in case of an unhappy encounter with a troublemaker somewhere along his route.

"There's no need for that," said the stranger, waving his hand in a half-circle as if to dismiss the club. The man's thumb and pinky finger touched as he gently motioned the weapon aside. Herb slowly dropped the bat on the ground, his mouth agape, his head turned curiously to one side.

"What ... what do you want with me?" Herb nervously eyed the man, noting his odd clothing and open sandals. Why would anyone wear open sandals on a cool April day?

"You are a fan of the idea of time travel, are you not?"

"Well, yes. Yes, I am." Herb remembered the book in his hand and held it up for the man to see as if he needed proof.

"You are a man of God too, are you not?"

Now, that question was a little personal coming from a stranger and Herb thought about his answer.

"I go to church."

"You go to church each week. You place a

generous offering in the plate, is this not true?"

"Yes. In fact, I donate the commissions on my first ten sales each week, but how would you even know to ask that?"

"You sit up front in church, so you can be surrounded by the lovely worship music of that impressive pipe organ and choir. You listen intently to every word from your minister, the Reverend Waller."

"Now, just hold on a minute. How do you know all this? Are you a spy of some sort? What do you want with me?" Herb's hands were at his hips, his body language demanding to know exactly what was going on. His thoughts raced. His imagination went into overdrive.

"I am not a spy, Herb. I am your Father."

"Now, hold on there, my friend. Now you're getting way out there. I know my father and you are definitely not my father. He lives over in Newtown and he's probably at the club playing cards right about now." Herb looked around to see if anyone was witnessing this bizarre encounter. A couple of kids by the pond appeared to be motionless. He thought about picking up the bat.

"Herb, I am your spiritual Father."

"What? You're *what*?" Herb's mind seemed to lose control. His hands began to shake.

"Do you believe in God?"

"Yes. Yes, I do." Herb proudly affirmed

his faith. His doubts were evident, and he was not terribly convincing.

"Do you believe in Jesus Christ as the Son of Man?"

"Uh, yes." This was getting very weird, very fast. Was it a test? Was it a dream?

"You believe, do you not, in the Holy Spirit?"

Herb just nodded, fear and wonder, and confusion wrapping him, now immobilizing him.

"Then I have chosen the right man. I am He, and I stand in front of you. I *am*."

Herb stumbled backward, catching the corner of the rear-view mirror on his head. His Magic Dairy hat fell to the ground. Perhaps and hopefully this was some weird dream. Maybe the milk was a bit sour or the leftover meat caused an unusual vision. He looked down and slowly picked up his hat, fully expecting and frankly hoping to be alone when he stood up again.

"Have you hurt yourself?" The gentle man inquired with some concern. All Herb could do was remember to breathe. He counted his inhalations. He tried to feel for a pulse. He thought he would panic and run, but instead, a peace settled over him, a strange peace unlike any he had ever known.

"You, are ... He?" Herb slowly looked up at the blue sky. It was as deep a blue as he could ever recall.

"I *am*," repeated the man, softly.

"Do you mind if I sit down? This is all just too strange for me to handle."

"Please sit. I know there is no easy way to reveal myself and so I seldom do. And of course, I'm making myself visible to you in a way that's familiar. I don't think you could handle three of us all at once." The man paused, a slight smile on his heavenly face. "Take a few deep breaths, and trust that what I tell you is real."

Herb did as was suggested and for a good full minute, then looked back. This person was indeed different, having not a glow to him, but almost, what was it, an aura about him. He would never be able to explain it. When the man moved, it was without visible effort; he simply appeared in the space he wished to occupy. Herb noticed he was still holding the book in his hand. He put down *The Time Machine* and took a deep breath, shaking his head as he exhaled.

"I'm sorry; you said something about time travel. You know it's a curiosity of mine. I mean, you can tell by this book, right?" There was only a nod in response.

"So, if you are ... God ... I guess you can travel anywhere and anytime you want, is that right?" Another nod.

"And you're going to show me how to do it?" A reassuring third nod.

"Let me explain," the spirit said. "Time to

you is clocks and schedules, calendars, aging, birth, death, and it runs your life. Your alarm clock measures the time and tells you when to go to work."

"Correct. That is time."

"To me, and to my mansion of souls, time does not exist in such a manner. To us, all things that have happened, or will happen, exist at once." Herb just shook his head. It sounded like the Reverend Waller trying to explain a concept from Revelations or some theoretical physicist from the University of Chicago.

"You know what a card catalog is, right?" Herb nodded. The Danbury library had a large card catalog.

"The card catalog shows you where to find different books, and gives you a reference number so you can go straight to it, right?"

"Yes." Herb still was not sure where this was going. He again nervously looked around.

"Don't worry, no one can see us, and time as you know it has stopped. Listen." Herb listened intently, trying to hear the birds, the wind, and the men working nearby. Nothing. Then he noticed the ringing in his ears had stopped. He looked at the man with wonder, tapping his ear with his hand. A big smile crossed his face.

"Your hearing problem does not exist if time has stopped."

"Go on." Herb was mostly convinced and wanted to learn more.

"I want you to think of eternity as one endless card catalog, from which you can logically select any card, representing any point in your understanding of time." To prove his point, time started again, and Herb's ringing of the ears started up. The men at the trampoline park were noisily taking their lunch break.

"Do you understand what I've explained to you?"

Herb nodded. It was so simple, it made sense. He wondered what came next.

"Think of it this way; the day of your birth is recorded on a card in this catalog, if you will, just as I have planned it, and the date of your earthly death is also recorded, on a different card." Herb didn't know what to say. The notion of his life being part of God's plan was well known to him, and millions of other believers. To have it laid out in such terms ... it finally made sense ... if indeed this was real and not a dream.

"I have chosen you, and I have given you this special truck to witness for yourself, what Mr. Wells hinted at in his book."

Herb shook his head as if to shake off the cobwebs of having deeply slept. The man was still there, patient and gentle. He looked at the book. What should he do?

"It is a lot to consider suddenly. I know

this. That is why I want you to think about it for a while. Pray. Share it with June." Herb smiled. He knew June. "It's alright to tell her. She will believe you." Herb said he would.

"Good. When you are ready, come back to this place, in this truck, and look for a card tucked into the spot here in the tree where the first limb branches out from the trunk." Herb saw the spot. "Your travels will take no time from your clock. It will appear to anyone who may notice that all you did was pick up a card."

"You will travel to a time that will be of significance to you, whatever comes to mind voluntarily or involuntarily at the instant you pick up the card and sit in the truck." Herb nodded side to side, a half-smile of skepticism crossing his lips.

"Have faith, son. This is my gift to you if you promise to learn from it."

At that moment, Herb looked towards the pond and noticed two boys fishing at the shoreline. He instinctively reached his hand out to shake the hand of the stranger who claimed to be God. At almost the same instant, he retracted his hand, wondering how he could be so brazen to try and touch the great I Am.

"It's alright. I understand." Herb felt as if a comforting arm encircled his shoulders, and instantly experienced peace.

"Will I see you again?" Herb had to know.

"When the time ... is right." A sly grin crossed the man's face. God had a sense of humor after all.

A breeze swept across the pond, causing ripples in the water. Herb saw the boys look over towards his truck. They did a double take. Herb looked back and the man was gone, a small manila card stuck in the crook of the elm tree's trunk the only sign that anything was different. In an instant, the card blew away on the breeze and disappeared. Herb stood alone for a moment, then cautiously climbed back into his truck, peering inside first to see if anything looked different or out of place.

As the little engine of the Divco milk truck chugged to life, the boys' attention was drawn to their fishing lines. Both bobbers disappeared with a jolt beneath the now-calm water. They had fish on the line! Reeling them in, they found two large perch on their hooks. The odds of catching a perch in the little pond were long; the odds of two of them catching perch this large, at the same exact moment, made no sense at all.

Chapter Ten

Not knowing what else to do, Herb put the new Divco into gear and headed back to Magic Dairy. It was indeed a chore to concentrate on the road and the tricky hand controls seemed awkward for some reason, but before long, he pulled into the Magic Dairy parking lot and began unloading the empties and sorting his notes on today's sales. As soon as those chores were done, Herb went to see if Mr. Mark had a moment. Betty, the secretary and gatekeeper for Frank Mark smiled when she saw Herb.

"You sure look happy for someone who just came in off the road."

"I do?" Herb wondered what he looked like after the fantastic encounter he'd just experienced.

"Yes, you do Mr. Lundy, and I don't think I've seen you smile that much in six months." Now, that comment made Herb want to check a mirror. He was smiling, serenely.

"Uh, can I see Mr. Mark for a moment?"

"I think now is a good time. Go right in."

Frank Mark's office was impressive but not outlandishly so. It was clear that he was in charge. One wall featured awards and certificates from various dairy associations, customers, and suppliers, and another wall had a shelf with several scale models of the assorted delivery trucks in use past and present by Magic Dairy. An oversized carved mahogany desk dominated the room and Mr. Mark's overstuffed executive chair completed the intimidating look.

"What can I help you with, Herb?" Frank Mark knew all his drivers by name, especially the war veterans.

"Well, I was wondering if it would be possible for me to switch trucks to the one I had today. My regular truck is in for service and I drove a brand new one today. I think it will help me sell more because I'll be able to do my routes faster. In fact, today I beat my old record on the south-side route by three minutes." Mr. Mark almost rolled his eyes thinking about Herb's penchant for timing himself. Instead, he just looked at Herb and pursed his lips.

"Well you know Herb, if I start showing any favoritism, especially for something like this, I'll be fending off requests all day long from the other drivers." Herb looked at his feet and thought about a good comeback.

"What if I could be assigned to that truck just a couple days a week, say maybe Monday and Thursday? Do you think that would be alright?"

Frank Mark thought about it. Herb was one of his very best drivers, always on time, never out of balance with his billing and collections, and a heck of a salesman.

"Tell you what. I think we could do that. Just a couple of days a week, probably no one will even notice. By the way, it's a funny thing about that new truck."

"What do you mean?" Herb was more curious than ever. He had been told the truck would be part of his time travel experience but had no clue why.

"I did not order that truck." Mr. Mark stood up from behind his desk. "In fact, it just showed up the other day from the Divco distributor. I called and told them I didn't order any new truck, and you know what he said?"

"Sorry, I have no idea."

"He said it had been ordered by an anonymous party, by mail, with specific instructions to paint it in the Magic Dairy livery, and there was a little gold-colored plate the buyer wanted to be affixed to the inside of the hood. Gave them a special tool as well. Darndest thing." Frank Mark shook his head and then gestured out the window. "So, I told the guy it made absolutely no sense, and you know what he said to me?"

"Keep it?" Herb offered his best guess.

"That's exactly what he said." Frank Mark slapped his hand on his desk for effect. "Said it was paid for in cash, everything was in order, and they even paid to ship it here. I just can't figure it out, but what the heck; if someone wants to donate a truck, who am I to argue?"

The truck donation made no sense to Frank Mark, but it did to Herb, though he dared not say why. If he had been in Frank's shoes, he'd have taken the free truck, too. "What about that gold ... thing?" Herb had an idea what it was for.

"Tell you what. Let's go look at it." And with that, both men walked out to the parking lot to pop the hood on the Divco. The hood was in two parts, hinged in the middle. No little gold plate on the left side. They moved to the other side of the truck.

"Well, I'll be. Look at that." Both men leaned forward. A two-inch gold-colored metal plate with a plain carved fish shape was indeed affixed to the inside of the hood. It had slightly rounded corners, four screw holes with a type of screw neither man had ever seen and was about half an inch thick. Both men stepped back.

"What do you think this is all about?" Mr. Mark had a quizzical look on his face. He reached out to rub the small plate and looked at Herb.

"I'm sure I don't know."

Chapter Eleven

With nothing else to accomplish, Herb hopped in his car and made the short drive home. Herb and June lived in a smallish cottage style home on Victor Street off Lake Avenue towards the western part of Danbury. It was a two-story home with a finished basement, two bedrooms, a living room, a kitchen, and a dining room, plus a full bath and half-bath downstairs. A short driveway curved around the home to a parking space behind the house. A clothesline that Herb had rigged up using two six-inch pulleys made hanging and retrieving laundry a cinch, even in cold weather. It stretched from just outside the back-kitchen door to a telephone pole forty feet away, perfect to hold two loads of laundry for June and Herb. A wicker basket held an assortment of clothespins.

Despite having stopped to talk with Mr. Mark and inspecting the truck, Herb was home earlier than usual. June was just finishing up her knitting of a hat and mittens for the church's mission outreach to an orphan's home in Chile. If she wasn't busy with something else, June was constantly knitting for the charity. It made her feel good to know her lovingly knitted hats, mittens, and sweaters would go to good use in the cold Andes Mountains homes of needy children and families. Herb was busting at the seams to tell June what had happened at the park but hesitated.

"How was your route today?" June was curious about why he was home early.

"Oh, it went pretty well. I had a new truck and I got out a little early, so I just pushed right through lunch and finished up my route."

"Did you set a new record?" June knew her man. Herb just laughed under his breath.

"Yes, I did. By three minutes."

"That's nice." It was a kind but throw away response. The type one makes when they're only half-listening.

Herb went to wash up. Staring at the mirror, he did notice a slightly different look about him, though it was not obvious what it was. Peaceful? Serene? Bemused? June had not looked up from her knitting so hadn't made a comment. Perhaps it was his imagination.

Since it was only Monday, there was no "homework" for Herb. Later in the week, he'd need to tally up all his orders, his regular sales, the extras he'd sold, and sum up the collections. June often helped and her second set of eyes had quietly saved Herb from reporting a mistake more than once. Her innocent questioning of an incorrect figure would let Herb keep accurate books without feeling as if he was being graded.

If his figures did not match what the main office had on record, there'd be trouble to pay, but Herb was only out of balance once, in his first year on the job, and it was because he'd transposed two figures on a large order at one of the big homes on Deer Hill Avenue. They ordered lots of extras for a holiday party, and in the rush of taking the order, he'd scribbled a few numbers that were officially recorded in error later. Other than that, his record was perfect, and he was proud of it. Other drivers who were not so attentive were disciplined or let go even if the out of balance situation became habitual. Herb wandered back to the living room.

"How about I take you to El Dorado tonight?" June look at Herb like his hair was on fire.

"What? Herb, it's Monday. Are they even open? Did you get a big bonus or something?"

"Or something. Yes, they're open." The idea of going out to eat on a Monday, much less a place so fancy as El Dorado was totally out of line for the normally frugal Lundy family, so June's reaction was well-founded.

"I'll tell you about it later." Except Herb could not bring himself to tell June what happened at Rogers Park by the pond under the elm tree. She would think he'd fallen absolutely and totally off his rocker. The man ... God ... had told him June would understand but still, Herb hesitated. He chewed his bottom lip, wondering.

"Oh, this came in the mail for you today. Very strange. It's just a plain manila card with no writing on the back. Just your name and address." June handed the card to Herb with a confused look. Herb's mouth fell open.

"I think we'll need to leave a little early and have a drink before dinner." June turned her head and raised an eyebrow. A drink on a Monday, at the El Dorado no less. Just what had happened today?

The restaurant was only a few blocks away, but for the Lundy's it may as well have been half a state away. Going to the El Dorado was pleasing to the palate but not kind to the wallet. June and Herb arrived and were escorted to a small, half-round booth in a quiet corner of the mostly empty establishment. It was early, and it was Monday, after all. The tufted red leather curved bench seat allowed for intimate small talk. The waiter smiled a fake smile and took their drink order; a glass of red wine for June and Ballantine Ale for Herb. Herb's beer arrived in a pilsner glass and the couple touched glasses together before sipping.

"Now, what's this all about?" June was patient but her interest was fully piqued. Herb hesitated. In his head, he heard, "Have faith." He breathed deeply and put his glass down, taking June's hand into his own.

"I ... I had a very unusual encounter today," Herb started. "I met a holy man."

"You mean a minister? Reverend Waller?"

"No, a very unusual man. He appeared next to me down at Rogers Park when I stopped to eat after I finished my wonderful record-setting run.

"What do you mean, he appeared?"

"I looked up, and this man was standing there. There was a sudden breeze that came out of nowhere, and then this man was just standing there next to the truck."

"That is strange." June paused and turned her head slightly, sipping her wine while she gazed out the window noticing an old pickup truck laden with yard debris laboring up Lake Avenue. "Are you OK?" June wondered if Herb had been working too hard. Perhaps spending some time at that bar down on Ives Street.

"I'm completely OK, don't worry. But this man ... he said he was ..."

"Said he was who?" June sat up in her seat and leaned forward. Herb took a drink, looked down, then directly into June's blue eyes.

"Jesus."

Chapter Twelve

It was Tuesday morning, and Herb was on time, as usual, to work despite tossing and turning most of the night. June had believed his story, brief as it was. She had faith in Herb until someone could prove him wrong. She slept peacefully while Herb fumbled fitfully to and fro, his mind bent on trying to absorb what had happened, and what was next. He needed to simply default to trust and faith but instead focused on a worldly explanation.

As expected, Herb was assigned his old truck, with new brakes, a new clutch, and no little gold plate under the hood. His route on Tuesday and Friday led him to the north of Danbury, way out on Pembroke Road, Padanaram Road, past the FCI, and up to New Fairfield along the back roads. He worked over to the New York border, and then back down to King Street, past Richter Park and West Lake Reservoir. West Lake was where I and my other fishing buddy Rick really liked to dip our lines more than anyplace else. Finally, Herb worked his way down over to Miry Brook Road and the Magic Dairy.

Although Herb had wanted to swing by Rogers Park just to see if there was a small manila card tucked into the big limb of the elm tree, he decided against it. He didn't have the special truck anyway, so what good would it do? A million questions ran through his mind the entire day, and while he was his usual efficient self on the north-side route, he was, as any reader might imagine, quite distracted. His sales reflected it, too. For one of the only times in the last year or so, he came back to the Dairy with a fair amount of unsold inventory.

"That's not like you," chimed the ever-cheerful "Bucko" Stevens, helping Herb unload the remains of the unsold cream, eggs, and cottage cheese.

"What are you doing here this time of day?" Herb was curious as to why Harry was still at the loading dock, some twelve hours after his shift began in the very early morning.

"Just filling in for today. It's no problem." Harry turned back to his work, waving to another driver coming in from his run.

"Hey, Herb!" Herb turned around to face Harry, now standing on the other side of the loading dock. His face looked serene.

"It's going to be OK. Don't worry. Everything's going to make sense." And he was gone, reaching inside the other truck, taking out the empties and putting the trays on the conveyor for the washroom.

Herb stopped in his tracks. What did Harry mean? Could he be talking about ... no, it didn't add up. He turned away for a moment and then turned back. He went over to ask Harry what he'd meant but Harry was gone.

"Have you seen Harry?" Herb asked one of the other drivers.

"Harry Stevens?"

"Yeah wise guy, Harry Stevens. Have you seen him?"

"What would Harry be doing here this time of day?" The man shook his head and turned back to his unloading work.

"Wasn't he just here helping you?"

"No," the man answered with growing impatience, "I'm unloading the truck myself unless you want to help." The man stopped lifting and looked at Herb curiously.

"No, that's OK, you finish. I'm going home." Things were getting more curious.

Herb Lundy did not go home. Instead, he headed over to a dark little bar on Ives Street near the railway station, parked his car and walked inside, leaving his Magic Dairy jacket and hat in his car. He knew the afternoon bartender by first name. They had served in the same outfit – the 392nd Bomb Group over in England in late 1944 and early 1945. Bob Waller was the Reverend Waller's cousin but did not obviously share the same depth of faith as the older Waller. It did not matter. Everyone knew Bob by the nickname, "Stache." His overgrown mustache flowed down well past the corners of his mouth and over his top lip.

"Ah, Mr. Lundy I presume. A hard day at the office?" Bob was nothing if not cheerful. A smiling and outgoing bartender earned larger tips even from close friends who knew the game.

"You could say that. How about a shot and a beer?" Herb needed a quick buzz, something to snap him back to reality, or what he thought was reality. Stache just rolled his eyes, serving up the Four Roses shot and Herb's Ballantine in one swift move.

"Thanks." Herb dumped the Four Roses into his beer and drank half the glass. He stretched his neck and rolled his head back and forth. The other patrons in the bar did not look up from their drinks.

"Better?" Stache tilted his head a bit as he eyed his old friend.

"Getting there." The bar was nearly empty except for a couple of rail workers at the other end and a younger guy checking out the song selection on the jukebox.

"Stache," Herb began, "Do I look any different to you?" Stache just looked at him. "No, really, do I look ... strange?"

"No stranger than usual, my friend. What's eating you?"

"I don't know." Herb ran his fingers through his hair, smoothing it back. "Something weird happened yesterday, and something today, too. I wonder if I'm going nuts."

"You wanna tell me about it?" Stache leaned over the bar counter grasping Herb's forearm with conviction and, looking Herb in the eye. Herb drank half of the remaining beer. He said nothing, looked down at the bar top and slowly shook his head.

"You and I go way back, Herb," Stache continued, softly. "I'm not gonna twist that arm of yours but you know you can tell me anything. After all we've been through." He left it there.

"No. No, I think I need to figure this one out for myself." Herb tried to convince himself.

"As you wish, my friend, as you wish." With that, Stache stood back up and turned his attention to the rail workers who signaled with an empty glass and a nod of the head they were each ready for a third draft beer.

Herb finished his drink, inhaled deeply and left two bucks on the bar. He slid off the barstool and stretched. He sighed deeply and strolled towards the door and daylight.

"Herb!" Stache called out as Herb reached the door. Herb half-turned to see what Stache wanted.

"It's going to be OK. Don't worry. Everything's going to make sense."

Chapter Thirteen

My West Lake fishing buddy, Rick and I had just walked out of Meeker's Hardware on White Street, right next to the railway station. Rick's dad needed some weird (to us) part for a lawnmower he was fixing so Rick and I volunteered to take a hike over to Meeker's. It wasn't all that far, and it was a nice April day. It was about that time for all men to attend to their mowers, especially those with gasoline engines. We headed there right after school.

Meeker's was a treasure; an old hardware store that had everything you could want if you could find it. All kinds of hand tools, saws, hammers, nuts and bolts, bins full of nails and screws, rope, copper tubing, pipe fittings, small motor parts, and thousands of other items nearly littered the store from ceiling to floor. Each aisle held loosely categorized and similar items, and although simply asking for what you needed was faster, the men and boys of Danbury often preferred to browse and tarry longer than necessary. For them, it was the equivalent to the ladies' Genung's store on Main Street, a distinctive shop for women who sought finer dresses and accessories, and from where I would purchase small gifts like winter gloves or a scarf for my mother at Christmas.

From the creaky wooden floors to the weathered countertop and cast of regulars who took habitat for hours at a time, Norman Rockwell himself could not have conceived a more rustic, New England-like edifice if he spent all day and a pipe-full or two trying.

Bag in hand, we turned left, heading towards Main Street for the walk home and had gone a couple of blocks when a maroon Ford sedan came flying out of Ives Street without a hint of stopping and roared down White Street towards the high school. Rick was reading the package label on the little muffler he'd just bought, and I had to pull him back from getting hit. A few of the words we'd learned from manual laborers around town came flooding out from each of us, at high volume. A stunned lady nearby gave us a look. Sheepishly, we increased our walking speed to a slow trot and looking away, turned the corner down Main Street.

Herb had no idea why he was heading east on White Street. He had to head somewhere and shortly after crossing the railroad tracks and passing by the big Leahy gas ball, he calmed down enough to mind the speed limit.

After a few blocks, he turned right onto Wildman Street and parked in front of his old house, across the street near the tracks. Maybe there was an answer there. It was here, with his friend Stan, he'd dreamed about distant places and other times. What was it like in the past? What would the future hold? It was easy enough to study the past and he'd leafed through all the Encyclopedia Britannica volumes more than once, absorbing tidbits of history that interested him. The copies his family had were old – printed before the First World War in fact – but contained all sorts of information that drove Herb's imagination. Roman legions, the Civil War. It was great to read about faraway places and times, but wouldn't it be great to be there, and then?

What about the future? What about rocket travel? Could man visit the moon; go further? What would science and technology bring in the next fifty years? Would cars really look as sleek as the ones depicted in Popular Mechanics? And what about eternity and the card catalog of endless time he'd been told about? What lessons awaited him? Would he finally understand what Reverend Waller was talking about?

Herb sighed. He had no choice but to believe. In fact, he embraced the belief that something quite special was about to happen. Thursday and the south-side route could not come quickly enough.

Chapter Fourteen

"The fruit of the Spirit is love ..."
-Galatians 5:22

Thursday. As promised, the brand new Divco truck with the little gold plate attached under the hood was assigned to Herb Lundy. Mr. Mark had come through. Herb hurriedly loaded the truck with milk bottles, cream, a few chocolate milk bottles, and some eggs for Mrs. Russell on Housman Street. He didn't forget. He tingled with excitement and couldn't wait for his lunch break at Rogers Park. After all, he had been told his trip in time wouldn't affect the current time. The entire period he was gone would not register on even the finest, most accurate Swiss-made clock. Herb headed for Bethel and his first run of stops along South Street and Coalpit Hill Road.

The early morning stops were ones where Herb simply took the empties out of the galvanized insulated boxes on the front step and replaced them with full milk bottles. It wasn't a good idea to walk in on a family just waking up and stuff their fridge. Sometimes there was a note in the box requesting extra milk, a bottle of cream, maybe some buttermilk. By 1957, some consumers had begun to buy skim milk; a byproduct of the butter-making process. Before marketing folks began convincing people they could lose weight by switching to the non-fat variety, the dairies simply threw it out or fed it to hogs or calves as a protein supplement. After all, who would ever pay for hog swill? With enough marketing dollars and a few well-placed doctor recommendations, it turns out that the American people would.

Herb was on automatic pilot, stopping at each home without thinking about it. Along the way, he spotted a car in the driveway of a home on Putnam Drive he knew had just been sold. He got out and left a flyer in the crease of the front door. He had to hustle for new customers, especially before the other dairies got to them. He'd remember to come back at a more welcoming hour to make introductions and close a deal. Working on a base salary and commission had its good points, but one always had to be building up one's business.

The morning flew by and Herb finished three-quarters of his route by 11:30. He steered the little Divco truck west towards Rogers Park, heading up the last steep hill on Newtown Road before bearing left onto Triangle Street. His route had taken him through Bethel continuing out on Plumtrees Road past Blue Jay Orchards, then across Old Hawleyville Road and connecting to Route 6, also known as Stony Hill Road in that part of town. Heading west back towards Danbury, he eyed the elegant Stony Hill Inn, home to many fancy banquets and weddings out by the gazebo and pond complete with stately swans. Herb whizzed by the Foredom Electric Company, where my dad worked, and finally made his way up the steep hill known as Newtown Road before veering left on to Triangle Street.

Now, the intersection of Newtown Road and Triangle Street was complicated by the fact that Newtown Road turned into White Street, and Beaver Brook Road which headed north also intersected at that same point, creating a wide, flat "X" in the road. It could be tricky to navigate if traffic was heavy, but at this hour, Herb was able to make an immediate left turn. He passed near his old house on Wildman Street, crossed the railroad tracks and was soon merging at the little triangle-shaped plot of land, on to South Street near the new Carvel store. A moment later, he turned left into Rogers Park and traveled the length of Memorial Drive, ending up under the elm tree by the pond. He turned off the Divco's engine, not daring to look at the tree.

Moments passed before Herb looked up to see the corner of a small manila card tucked into the crook of a large limb. He breathed deeply. But wait, shouldn't he have his lunch before embarking on whatever adventure he was going to undertake? Yes, that sounded right.

"No sense traveling through time on an empty stomach," he thought. Eating his tuna sandwich, Herb looked at the manila card tucked into the crook of the tree limb and sighed. What if it didn't work? Was he brave enough to go through with it? He silently downed the last of his sandwich, chased by a large gulp of milk. If he was going to do it, then he'd better get to it.

Herb looked around and saw no one who might spot him. A cool breeze quickened for a few moments; ripples formed on the pond and the wind swished through the spring leaves on the elm tree. Herb grasped the card in his hand. There was no writing on it, but he didn't expect any. What he was not sure of was "when" he was going to. It was in his unconscious or subconscious, perhaps. At least, he knew he didn't have any specific date in mind.

Taking a deep breath, Herb stepped inside the truck and at that point, everything became white. No sound, no movement, just a sense that everything was white. And then, it was over.

The Messerschmitt ME-109 was making a lateral run at the heavy B-24, coming from the left and slightly higher than the bomber, aligned as it was on the outside edge of the so-called combat box, a strategic formation that offered maximum protection for the lumbering planes. *Guts N' Glory* was the outside plane in the high element, leaving it vulnerable to attacking fighters approaching from the high 9 o'clock position.

In a second or two, the pilot would open up with machine guns and that devastating new 30mm cannon, trying to tear up the plane and with any luck, kill everyone on board. Herb Lundy instinctively re-cocked the Browning .50-caliber gun, preparing to fire at the marauder. He wouldn't need to lead the plane; it was coming straight at him. He felt his shoulder rub up against his old pal, Sergeant Withers, the other waist gunner. They glanced briefly at each other. Herb remembered his face, even obscured by the oxygen mask and helmet as if it were yesterday. It was, in fact, yesterday; many yesterday's ago.

The ME-109 pilot had only a few seconds to fire his weapons before streaking past the enemy bomber. He pressed the triggers. Nothing. A half-second later, he tried again. Everything jammed. At that moment, the pilot's eagerness to destroy the American plane switched to terror as he came in range of the waist gunner's .50-caliber machine gun. But nothing happened. No gunfire. A moment later, he streaked past the bomber, looking at the waist gunner, waving a half-salute at the stranger before veering off and out of the formation of bombers. For some reason, the pilot's life had been spared. He didn't care why.

Herb held the handles of his gun, his thumb touching the trigger, but he didn't shoot;

he couldn't shoot. The German pilot's guns had frozen up; either that or he ran out of ammo. It didn't matter. What mattered to Herb was that he had not done his job, to shoot at enemy planes and hopefully to shoot them down. He looked at his gloved hands. He felt the cold air on the edges of his face. He instantly wondered why his first trip through time would take him back to an unremembered battle in 1944.

Lieutenant Danforth got on the interphone. "Uh, waist gunner, why didn't you shoot at the 109?" No response. "Herb?"

"Yeah Skip, I don't know what happened. I was expecting him to shoot, and when he didn't, I didn't shoot, either. I guess I froze up." A long pause.

"Roger. Test-fire a few rounds. Make sure that thing works."

Herb did as he was told, aiming the Browning down and away from the formation. Brat ... brat-brat. It worked. The question on his mind; why didn't HE work?

Crossing the English Channel, the B-24 quickly approached England, the distant white cliffs a welcome sign to every Allied aviator. Dipping below 8,000 feet, the order came to doff oxygen masks and prepare for landing. Other than the failure to fire incident, the mission had been something of a "milk" run. No planes lost, only a few men with minor wounds among the twenty-nine bombers sent out. On any day, that was a major victory for the 392nd.

Herb's plane was one of the first to land. He looked out at the still-familiar landscape as the B-24 descended, finally landing at Wendling then idling over to its hardstand. Lieutenant Danforth skillfully guided the plane to the revetment and shut down engines. The crew got out, stretched, and hopped on a waiting jeep for debriefing. Herb's hometown buddy, Bob Waller was driving. They exchanged a wave and one of those mutual nods of relief where you raise your eyebrows greeting your friend who survived another mission and didn't have to say a word.

What on earth would Herb tell them? "Oh hey, I've just come back from 1957" ... or, "Hey, I'm a milkman now, what about you guys?" It was sure good to see some of the old faces, though. He felt that kinship, that brotherhood he had not experienced since those days, more than twelve years ago. Or was it all happening at once? Was he in 1945 and 1957 at the same time? What WAS time? He thought of the unending card catalog that had been explained to him only days ago. Or was it just now? Either way, the feeling of camaraderie was comforting; it was at the same time reassuring and peaceful. He loved these men. He wished he had told them.

It was a quick debriefing. Bombs were on target, flak was light and inaccurate, and the few fighters they encountered were mostly ineffective. A "milk" run, indeed, said the major. Herb softly chuckled at the use of the term, given how he now made a living.

"Something you want to say, Sergeant Lundy?" The intelligence officer was not amused, despite the fact he'd have an easy debrief with every crew today, leaving more time to enjoy a pint or two in nearby Beeston at the Oaken Barrel pub. Herb just shook his head. "I understand you missed an open shot at a ME-109, is that correct?" How did the major know that? In fact, Herb didn't remember any such incident happening on any of the missions he'd flown; it must not have been meaningful to him at the time or perhaps was simply lost in the long chain of missions.

"Yes sir, he was coming directly at me but did not fire. I hesitated for some reason, and just like that, he was gone."

"I see." The major paused, thinking. Had the circumstances resulted in injury to men or damage to the aircraft, he might have had a stricter response. He chose to be gentle on the veteran aviator. "Try not to let it happen again." Herb murmured an assurance and looked down at his shoes. All at once, a deep wrenching feeling of remorse overcame Herb for the men he had killed in combat; for the bombs dropped on people below. It was a dirty job that had to be done, and he was proud of doing his part to stop

72

the Nazi regime, but at his core, he still carried guilt for the deaths he'd caused. He felt a small moment of joy however, for the life of the German pilot he'd let pass by. It was almost as if that one life made up for the others. Herb thought back to the many missions he had flown and while some of them were etched into his memory, try as he might, Herb could not recall an incident or mission where he failed to do his job. Was a time warp somehow changing the circumstances of a long-ago flight? Was it simply a parallel event or one of several possible alternatives that could have occurred in the same mission? The possibilities were mystifying.

A few moments passed. The major asked a few final routine questions that Herb did not hear; his mind was swirling. In response to being spared by the German pilot's failed equipment, he had returned the favor, consciously or not, with an act of mercy, or was it an act of love, during a bloody conflict. The pilot seemed to know it, waving at him as he sped past.

No medals were awarded for NOT shooting at the enemy, nor was there a specific law against showing what amounted to mercy, or love, but inside, while he still harbored guilt and remorse for his other collective deeds, Herb felt a comfort he hadn't known before and a sense of peace. Without bothering to dissect his feelings any further, Herb settled on this: as a comrade-in-arms, albeit under a different flag, as one man to another forced into a deadly circumstance, he loved the German pilot who had not shot at him, and for whom Herb had returned the favor. He knew not why.

With nothing left to interrogate, the major announced to the crew they were dismissed. Everyone stood at half-attention and turned to leave. Herb was the last to stand, and as he did, he touched the manila card in his pocket, and everything went white.

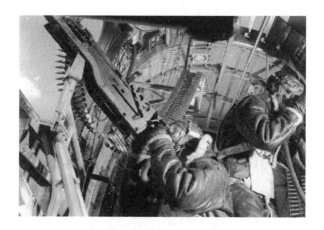

Chapter Fifteen

Sunday school at the First Congregational Church got out a little early because Mrs. Watson forgot her lesson plan and we spent the time trying to memorize the names of all sixty-six books of the Bible. Exactly how young kids wanted to spend Sunday morning. I was pretty good with the New Testament although I'd often get stuck at Colossians. Forget about the Old Testament – I could remember up to Ruth and that was it. I suppose I wasn't focused, or properly motivated. At any rate, we were quietly let into the sanctuary in mid-sermon as Reverend Waller went on about some passage from the book of Galatians. Something about the fruit of the Spirit.

I snuck into the pew next to my dad and looked around the big room dominated by the pipe organ. The choir was led by our mayor and they had on plain-looking but somewhat elegant black and white choir robes, waiting patiently for the last hymn. I saw one couple alone in the front row; the same people that were usually there every Sunday.

Herb Lundy held his wife's hand the entire service. He'd told her about the brief trip through time and frankly, was a little underwhelmed. After all, he had intimately known that time period, having lived it already, and thought he'd have access to any time period he could imagine. It was still a mystery how that date and event was chosen; he hadn't selected it consciously, and he had not been briefed on how to return. It was by chance – or was it – that he touched the manila card at the right moment and returned to the present. All of this was on Herb's mind.

He wasn't following the sermon very well, his mind occupied with his first trip in the Magic Dairy milk truck. After all, it was quite bizarre to even think such a thing was possible, much less experience it in person. Hey, H.G. Wells thought the adventures of time travel made a good book. Why not Herbert Edward Lundy? But still, if simply revisiting past events in his lifetime was going to be the extent of this adventure, Herb was slightly nonplussed. At that moment, he looked up to the reverend, pausing for effect in mid-sentence. He looked down at Herb and put special emphasis on his next words.

"Have FAITH … in your belief. Put your TRUST in almighty God, and your needs shall be answered." As the reverend continued his thoughts, his eyes focused elsewhere, Herb nodded to himself. Reverend Waller, the reverend's cousin Stache, and Harry Stevens had all given him words of encouragement, words bound in faith. Why he had no idea. It was the reverend's job to provide such encouragement, but the other two … it made no sense. Then Herb knew … he was not alone on this journey. He had friends to help him along. Angels, perhaps.

At the Main Street Bake Shop after church, my sister and I waited at the counter to order our dozen hard rolls. I saw Mr. Lundy the milkman come in the store but this time, he did not simply grab his bag and leave. He made a point to find Stan and eagerly shook his hand and grabbed his shoulder. The two chatted for a few moments, smiling and laughing. Customers shifted their weight and checked their watches while the old friends talked for a moment or two. I could hear them promising to get together later that week for some reason or other. Herb stopped at the checkout stand and spoke to the girl there. She reached below the counter and pulled out a slip of paper. Herb took his wallet out of his back pocket and handed over some bills, making sure to pay his tab in full.

The seasons changed gradually in Western Connecticut. Summer did not suddenly turn to fall, and spring would tease us, sometimes for weeks before coming into flower. Herb thought of this while driving to work in the pre-dawn hours Monday morning. He felt within him the slightest change. He wasn't abruptly moving from one season in his life to another, but a faint, barely perceptible shift in his attitude was noticeable. He felt it must be related to his time trip the other day. Today, he'd try another one, although "when" it would take him, and why, he could not fathom a guess.

This would be the third overall route in the new Divco; it even had a new smell to it, which would certainly wear off after the first spilled milk soured in the midday sun. No matter, it wasn't the newness or the smell; it was what this Magic Dairy truck could do.

The route today was mostly uneventful except for the fact that Herb kept thinking about how to control – if he could – the date and maybe the time he wished to visit. It couldn't just be a random thing, captured from the far reaches of his memory, or imagination – or could it? Occupied and distracted by this, he almost forgot to deliver Mrs. Hack's special order of cream. In a hurry, Herb nearly burst through her kitchen door on Grand Street, said a quick hello to the coffee-sipping Mrs. Hack, stuffed two bottles of milk in her fridge and grabbed the empties as he said a quick goodbye. No small talk today. As he stepped back into the truck, Mrs. Hack called out to him from her porch for her bottle of cream.

"Oh, shucks! Sorry, Mrs. Hack, I guess I'm kind of distracted today."

"Just take a deep breath, Mr. Lundy," she scolded in a faintly Irish accent. "You don't want to get yourself hurt; you know."

The South Street School needed service today, and that took a good ten minutes, including a brief chat with the assistant principal who happened by the cafeteria and was in a talkative mood. The sound of a history lesson being taught and children's voices in response were music to Herb's ears. Some story about World War I is what it sounded like. These things hadn't seemed remarkable any of the hundreds of other times he'd visited the school.

Extracting himself from the conversation, Herb guided the truck past Bothelo's Barber Shop and the little candy store nearby, taking a left on to Town Hill Avenue, working his way up the hill, then back down around the block on Stone Street, working his stops, ending up at the little grass triangle where he merged on to South Street. He couldn't help but notice a small crowd at the Carvel ice cream shop across the street. Even on a late morning in April, the new store was doing quite a trade. He made a mental note to stop by and try a soft-serve cone on his way to Bethel later.

Herb Lundy made the familiar turn on Memorial Drive, past the War Memorial building on the left and the rose trellises, and then continued without stopping to Rogers Park pond, settling the Divco under the elm tree. As expected, a manila card was tucked into the same spot on the tree. Herb wondered if the card determined the place and date, or if it simply opened the door to his adventure. Herb sighed deeply. He'd soon find out.

There were a couple of workers on the adjacent soccer field, and it looked like they were putting down lines on the field. It was time for soccer matches to start up again. No matter, they were too occupied with their work to care about a milk truck parked under an elm tree. Where and when would he go today, and what would he find? The notion was beyond exciting. A breeze kicked up over the pond. Herb pulled the card from its spot on the tree and stepped back into the truck, and just as it had the first time, everything went white.

Chapter Sixteen

Ever since I could remember, I had recurring dreams of two particular circumstances: riding in a car over a rickety wooden bridge on the verge of it giving way beneath us, and falling through the sky and seeing vividly the oddly and unevenly sized squares, rectangles, and geometrically random shapes of farmlands below. In this dream, I rushed downwards towards the brown and green fields and the carefully arranged stone fences. In my falling dream, I never reached the ground. In my bridge dream, the car never fell through the weak wooden beams, but I revisited each dream again and again.

The dreams would come to me with no particular frequency nor as a result of any circumstance I could remember, although they would come more often and be more likely to occur if I was sick with a fever. I had no point of reference for them. I had never been up among the clouds, presumably in an airplane, and so had no way to know what it looked like to be falling from the sky, and I had no awareness of any rickety old bridge.

I was aware of a conscious aversion to traveling over bridges but had no specific recollection of any wooden bridge, and since I was a passenger and not a driver, it mattered not, yet the scary bridge dreams continued.

These dreams confused me, not only because of the mysterious content but also the fact that they came to me again and again. I was mildly troubled, though not to the point of being tormented or distracted, and after being awake for a while, my mind became occupied with the other things that dwell in a boy's mind – marbles, toy soldiers, homemade gravity-driven go-karts, playing baseball, building models of old cars and of course, fishing. The significance of my dreams, especially the one where I would fall from the sky, though quite real, was somewhere down the list of my concerns. Being that young and insulated I had no notion of the concept of reincarnation or past life experiences nor would I for years to come. When it did come, in the form of the book, "Many Lives, Many Masters," I was willing to give that possibility a chance. If time came in slices, and I could access them somehow, well, why not leave that open to consideration?

Chapter Seventeen

"The fruit of the Spirit is joy..."

Herb Lundy rubbed his eyes. A thoroughly unfamiliar sight greeted him, that of an angular wooden building with a tin roof that was long and shallow in the front, and steep and much shorter in the back. A large metal pipe served as a chimney of sorts, belching smoke into the azure South Carolina sky. In the distance, Herb could see workers in the fields – black men and women, children maybe – either weeding or picking a crop, he couldn't tell for sure.

The wooden building was someone's home, and on the porch, a stout woman was busily peeling potatoes for tonight's supper and a man, perhaps her husband, was at work mending a crude-looking tool of some sort.

A few hundred yards away, a two-lane highway divided the fields – they were vegetable fields it appeared – and every now and then an old car would come into view, puttering down the road to a destination unknown. A low billboard announced to drivers that a visit to nearby Charleston was a great idea. Herb smiled to himself. He had grown up with cars like these. An old Model-T Ford, plus a sturdy looking pickup truck with wooden-spoke wheels and a homemade stake bed on the back piled high with picked produce. There went a classy Duesenberg, the kind with an open-air chauffer's seat and an elegant, enclosed cab for the obviously rich passengers, probably on their way to Florida. What great cars they were! And they looked to be in wonderful condition for being thirty-plus years old. But then Herb reminded himself he was visiting not only a place but a time. Heck, these vehicles were new.

He was in another time that was within his lifetime, that much was evident, but he would have been a very young boy, if not an infant. Keeping an open mind, Herb decided to see why he was sent here. He hadn't chosen it, that he knew of, but he was sure there must have been a good reason.

"Those are some cars, eh?" The voice startled Herb as he swung around to find its source. Charles Roosevelt Calvin stood tall and lean in his spanking-clean aviator's uniform, the kind with a high tunic neck and made from a heavy and uncomfortable looking woolen material. Herb figured the man to be a lieutenant by the insignia and a pilot too, by the wings on his chest. A young man, he couldn't have been more than twenty-three years old, maybe younger. A few medals adorned the space above his left chest and a colorful Croix de Guerre held a place of honor alone on his right.

"Ah, the Croix de Guerre caught your eye I see. Yes, sir, that's a French medal. I got it for shooting down three Fokkers in one day. And what a day that was." The man beamed a wide, white smile, made all the whiter by the dark brown skin of the man.

"Swell." Herb thought to himself. "I've gone back in time again and to another war, or another war era." He looked down at his shoes and sighed, then decided he was a passenger on this trip, and to simply be thankful for the opportunity. He looked up.

"Herb Lundy," he stuck out his hand.

"Charles Calvin," came the reply, "At your service." Another broad and welcoming smile as he bowed slightly to the stranger.

"I'm a bit confused, "Herb said. "I'm not sure why I'm here, and frankly, why you're here, either. Do you know?"

"Well, let's talk about it, but first, let me introduce you to my family."

Belle Calvin watched carefully over the picking fields from her rocking chair on the front porch. Peeling potatoes with skill and speed, she kept a wary eye on the workers, ready to shout to them with corrective instruction should they be slack in their work.

"That's my mama, Belle," said Charles. "She's a tough one, but I do miss her loving arms." The comment took Herb by surprise. Why would Charles say he missed her when he was right here? Unless.

"And that there, that's my daddy, George. He's worked this property for oh, thirty-five years I reckon. Since before I came 'round that's for certain."

"Charles," Herb interrupted. "Can they not see you? I mean, we're standing right here."

"No sir, Mr. Lundy, they can't see either one of us. I'm dead and all, and you, well you're from some other time, ain't ya?" Herb sighed while Charles smiled.

"How did you know that?"

"Oh, I'm supposed to show you this here scene, but I don't really know why. It's nice to see my family though." He smiled broadly and looked fondly upon his dear mama.

Herb pondered the moment. Given what he experienced in the last week, nothing much surprised him at this point.

George and Belle were having an animated conversation oblivious to the invisible and silent intruders while Charles and Herb stood on the porch listening.

"You about finished fussin' with that thing because you know I need some greens picked for dinner." George just shrugged.

"You gonna go to the garden or do I have to?" Belle held up her peeling tool and gave George that look.

"Yes'm," was the only response George could muster. It was a useful word; one he'd practiced and perfected for a variety of needs. He put down his work. Herb thought the wooden tool with a turning handle was for separating cotton from the seeds, sort of a manual cotton gin, and Charles agreed it was so. There must be cotton fields, too.

"So, do you know why I'm here?" Herb was still confused. Charles slowly shook his head indicating Herb would have to find out for himself.

Presently, the children came in from the field to wash up as Belle cooked her potato recipe along with collards and a freshly killed chicken from the barn. It was good, hearty food; plain but enough of it to feed a hungry family. Inside the wood slatted-floor cabin, Herb looked around and took in the simple surroundings – a bedroom for Belle and George and one for the children. A raised floor for what served as the kitchen and a small cross near the fireplace, plus a well-crafted table where everyone could sit together and share a meal. The only indulgence Herb could see was a large family Bible carefully nestled on its own handmade wooden stand.

The bathroom was an outhouse; a hand pump stood over the large porcelain sink serving as the source of cold well water. It was as simple a home as one could imagine, unencumbered by electricity or a telephone. There was no car or truck outside, no galvanized box for milk deliveries. Yet not a single complaint arose from the assembled family. In fact, laughter and joy permeated the room as children told tall tales to their adoring father and he smiled back at them with patient and loving eyes.

In a corner of the kitchen near the paned window stood a photograph of someone in uniform. A dried palm frond, the kind you get on Palm Sunday was attached to a corner of the frame. Upon closer examination, Herb recognized that it was Charles, his image lovingly preserved where all the family could see.

"Oh, I guess I can tell you." Charles' voice stunned Herb a bit, recalling him from his survey of the home.

"You see, when I was about seventeen, I got hold of a magazine that had a big article about flying in an airplane. Talked about the Wright Brothers and all and said how airplanes would be taking a big part in the Great War going on over in Europe. Well, I knew right away I wanted to fly. Real bad, I did."

"So, how is it that a young black man from South Carolina became an Army pilot?"

"Well, a year or so went by and of course our Army didn't have a lot of opportunities for a black man, so I got a ride into Charleston one day and came across a place where they were recruiting men to fly with the Escadrille. That's French for flying force, you know. "

"Yes, I'm familiar with the term."

"So, this one guy says we don't want his kind, but another man said no, wait. Let's take a look. And they did. They checked me out really good, including my eyesight and that's when they got excited."

"They got excited about your eyesight?" Herb made a face.

"Yes sir, they did. Said I had twenty fifteen eyesight which didn't mean much to me at the time, but in the end, it meant I could see extra good, and that's what they wanted in their pilots. So, they took me."

"The French Army."

"Well, an American working with the French Army but yes and off I went to France. They taught me to fly and shoot at a training base in Châteauroux and before I knew it, I was in the thick of the war."

"You said you shot down three Fokkers in one day."

"I did for sure, and I got a bunch more of them too before they got me."

"What happened?"

"Well, the Germans had a name for me. It was *Schwarze Katze*. I don't remember exactly, but it meant black cat. And word was, they had a bounty on my head. One day three of us were coming back from a patrol heading for our base south of Verdun and this red tri-wing Fokker came diving out of the sun at me. Shot my Nieuport up really bad and set my engine on fire."

"That must have been awful."

"Well, I wasn't gonna burn to death, so I just jumped out. I'd rather die falling than burning."

"No parachute?"

"That's right. The higher-ups thought if we wore a parachute, we'd bail out at the first sign of danger. Some of the pilots took their sidearm with them in case the plane caught on fire, you know, to end it that way."

Herb just shook his head slowly back and forth. He looked up at Charles.

Charles continued. "You know what I remember the most before I died?"

"What?"

"All those shapes of the farms. Some of them were square, some of them were rectangles, and some were oddly formed, but I remember them clearly, and the greens and brown colors and stone fences coming up at me fast. Then all I saw was a white light."

Herb thought for a moment. He was intimately familiar with the patchwork landscape of European farm country, having flown over it thirty-five times. Thousands of his 8th Air Force comrades had fallen to their deaths or parachuted into captivity or were killed by angry civilians. He thought it must have been awful to fall to your death, but then again, maybe not as bad as burning; at least there was a final view.

"It wasn't so bad," Charles continued. "I had time for a prayer on the way down. I was scared and all, but I put myself in the Lord's hands and knew I was OK."

The men turned to watch supper being served. Before anyone touched a morsel, they bowed heads and held hands, George leading them in a prayer of thanksgiving for the bounty they were about to receive.

George reminded the children to attend to their books after supper. His admonition was met with a few groans but no other obvious objections, knowing full well a sharp rebuke awaited the one who complained.

"Charles."

"Yes, Mr. Lundy."

"Your family has very little. No car, no conveniences. There's hard work to be done. Why are they so happy?"

"You don't know?"

"Why are they so happy?" Herb bowed his head a bit as he slowly repeated himself.

"You see those fancy cars going down the road?"

"Yes, of course."

"You see a fancy car outside this house?"

"No."

"Is my family wearing fancy clothes?"

"No, they're not."

"Do you see one of them telephones? Do you see an electric light?"

"I do not."

"Then it ain't things or money that makes 'em happy, is it?"

Herb thought a moment. He thought about his own possessions – his home, his car, his closet full of clothes, and his good job. He thought about the expensive restaurant he took June to the other day. Did those things make him happy?

Herb slowly nodded his head and looked at Charles. He understood. The family had very little in the way of money or valued property, but they had each other, they were comfortable within themselves, envious of no one, full of the knowledge they were who they were called to be. No doubt about it; they knew true joy.

They embraced their moment, and without a doubt knew of their salvation by the blood of Christ. It was taught to them in plainness; they lived quiet but honorable lives, and eternity with the Lord was theirs, as sure as the food on the table. Of this, there was no doubt and woe to anyone who tried to tell them otherwise. What they believed and how they chose to view the world had no monetary value, and no amount of money could earn it. Such was their contentment and their joy.

Herb rolled his eyes a bit as he thoughtfully pondered what he saw. It was not about comparing themselves to the rich folks driving past their home on the way to Florida in their expensive cars with their designer suitcases. The Calvin family knew that such comparisons and envy would rob them of their happiness and their joy. It was not about them; it was about Him.

Herb turned to Charles who smiled once more, and with a nod and friendly salute and big smile was simply no longer there. Herb listened to the lively and happy discussion at the table for another moment then touched the manila card in his pocket and everything turned to white.

Chapter Eighteen

"The fruit of the Spirit is peace..."

Waking suddenly from his deep slumber, Herb looked over at the old Luna bedside clock, its glow-in-the-dark radioactive hour and minute hands indicating he still had five minutes before it was time to get up. He set his head back on the pillow. Was today Tuesday? Was he in his own home? June's steady breathing assured him he was. Herb sighed deeply.

His two trips through time had taken him back to his late teens and also to a time he would be too young to remember. Both trips held a significance he recognized but could not yet fully assimilate. He had seen himself show mercy to an enemy. He had witnessed a family that was content and joyful despite having few material things and little hope of gaining them.

Herb thought about church. Did he really understand Reverend Waller's lessons or was he like some of the others, just there for the show? Somewhere inside, he felt like a strong new foundation was being poured, and he was pleased. Reaching over, Herb canceled the soft buzzing alarm before it could go off and went downstairs to make coffee.

Finishing the second cup of Maxell House

and two slices of buttered toast, Herb idly perused yesterday's late edition of the newspaper, not really absorbing what he was reading, simply turning the pages out of habit. What about traveling to the future? Was that in one of those little manila cards? He hoped so, trying to imagine life fifty years from now, a hundred maybe. What would Danbury be like? Would there really be flying cars? Would the new polio vaccine really work? Who would be president? Putting his coffee mug in the sink, Herb grabbed his Magic Dairy jacket and stepped outside into the brisk morning air.

Our house had one of the galvanized insulated milk boxes on the front step though I never thought much about it. My mom was not fond of the idea of a milkman just strolling into the house and anyway, our delivery was early in the morning, like before seven o'clock. What I looked forward to more was delivery from the Charles Chips guy. Every so often this wonderful man would deliver a big yellow tin of crisp, tasty potato chips. The funny thing is, we always seemed to run out well before the next delivery. Six people into one Charles Chips tin did not equate to a long-lasting snack. Not at our house.

Heading out the front door to play marbles with my neighborhood buddies one Saturday morning, I noticed a brand-new milk box on the front step. Instead of Marcus Dairy, this box had a logo for Magic Dairy. Milk is milk and I really didn't give it a second thought.

Buoyed by the recent time trips, plus the mild spiritual awakening Herb was experiencing, the savvy milkman's step was just a bit livelier on Tuesday morning. He smiled a bit even in the chilly pre-dawn hour at the loading dock. Oh, not that he never smiled, it was just that this smile seemed a bit more natural, at least it seemed that way to Harry Stevens. Harry thought he even heard a soft, whistled tune coming from Herb as he loaded the ice bags. Harry nodded to himself with quiet satisfaction, though he wasn't quite sure why. Something mysterious was going on. He knew it; he felt part of it, but all the details eluded him like he was a child trying to catch falling snowflakes on his tongue.

Herb's route was a long and winding affair, in an older Divco truck that steadfastly refused to climb any hill at the posted speed limit. Herb had to gauge his approach, gun the motor and use whatever momentum he could gather to climb the more challenging hills, and there was plenty to climb today. Herb guided the Divco down Ridgebury Road toward Ridgefield, stopping along the way to make his deliveries, veering off here and there into the surrounding neighborhoods. Like much of western Connecticut, the roads were lined by canopies of trees, scattering the early morning light and making Herb feel as if he were driving through a long, green tunnel. It was a peaceful time of day, one that he treasured.

Once in Ridgefield, Herb stopped at Ida's Café to make his delivery and to pick up a coffee to go and a hard roll with butter. Taking his mid-morning snack, Herb guided the little Divco truck around to Veteran's Park, where every Fourth of July a great fireworks display was held to the delight of children and their parents.

The crunchy roll needed the butter, and the coffee, too, to wash it down. It was good but not as good as the rolls at the Main Street Bake Shop. Finishing his snack, Herb slipped the Divco into reverse gear, checked his mirrors and began to back up.

Whack! A loud thud and Herb jammed on the brakes. There was nothing there a moment ago. He killed the motor and got out to see the damage. Nothing behind the truck, nothing on the ground. Looking up, he saw the source of the thud – the same man who visited him at Rogers Park. Jesus. Or God. Or an angel. He just wasn't sure. Herb's mouth opened but no words came forth.

"You have been busy," said the man, sizing up Herb as he spoke. Herb tried to mouth a response but could not speak.

"It's alright. I understand. So, you've been to the past and you've learned a thing or two."

"Uh, well yes, I think I have," Herb said nervously, not quite sure of himself.

"And what have you learned, Herb?"

Herb looked at the man's sandals and then looked up.

"I don't think money is going to buy me joy," said Herb, surer of himself.

"It is hard for a rich man to enter the kingdom of heaven. It is easier for a camel to go through the eye of a needle than for a rich man to enter the kingdom of God."

Herb recognized the parable of the needle from the Gospels. He nodded.

"Hard but not impossible." Herb was trying to find the loophole. What was "rich" anyway? Was it having a big bank account? Was it owning a warehouse full of things?

"Do you remember this? Blessed are the poor in spirit, for theirs is the kingdom of heaven." The man smiled. Pride of authorship, no doubt.

"I've wondered about that," said Herb, completely forgetting the melting ice in his truck.

"Does it mean only a poor man can go to heaven?"

"I get asked that a lot. I said, 'poor in spirit,' not poor as in having no money."

"Do you mean lacking spirit?"

"No Herb, what it means is that those who acknowledge that despite any worldly belongings, or any measure of wealth, they must find their way to depend on God to achieve their blessing; their deep-rooted happiness. Their joy. A worldly treasure means nothing compared to God's blessing. You can have a treasure, but without God, you have nothing. You must be poor spiritually; you must realize the need for and rely on God and not depend only on yourself or the world."

Herb leaned on his truck. He heard the crinkling sound melting ice makes as it shifts inside the ice bags.

"So, a rich man can go to heaven, but it's not likely such a man would rely on someone else, even God." Herb thought of some of the wealthy folks who lived on Deer Hill Avenue. He thought he understood. He suddenly pitied them.

"It's not likely. One with wealth is often in love with money, not his Father."

"The love of money is the root of all evil," Herb chimed in, lightly moving his head side to side as if he was revealing something to the statement's author. They both nodded, almost whimsically.

Herb noticed nothing around them was moving. No cars, no breeze rustling the leaves in the trees. No sound.

"Yes, Herb, this conversation is happening but it's not taking up any time." By now, Herb was growing more comfortable with the notion of time or rather, eternity. "Enjoy your next trip. I think you'll enjoy it."

And with that, the man was gone, and the sound of a honking car horn snapped Herb back to the present moment. A bird chirped. A distant truck horn blared.

"Hey, you almost backed into me! Why don't you watch where you're going?" An angry driver in a dark blue '56 Ford sedan was waving his rolled-up newspaper at Herb. Herb gave the man a warm, apologetic smile that calmed him so that he put down the paper and tipped his cap to Herb as he drove away. Herb thought about his encounter. Poor in spirit, rich in God's blessings. Money was not a factor; it came, and it went. What could it mean? Herb sighed deeply and felt more serene and relaxed than at any time in his life. He thought he knew the answer: peace.

Certainly, Herb had known war. The terrors, the madness of it all. He had called out to God on many occasions, mostly when he thought his life was about to end. Now he was being gently guided to his own serenity, his own peace. Huh.

Chapter Nineteen

Wednesday came and Herb ventured out as usual in one of the older Divco trucks. Herb's route took him to the north and east, past Brookfield and all the way to New Milford and later down to Newtown. The leg into Newtown was sparsely populated but had several good customers and Herb didn't mind the drive. He liked to take a break along the banks of the Housatonic River, especially in spring when it ran high and fast with the last of the melting snow. The sounds it made were both relaxing and invigorating at the same time.

The upper reaches of the Housatonic were a combination of creeks and streams, some fed by reservoirs and ponds in the Pittsfield Massachusetts area and beyond. The river twisted and turned its way down into Connecticut paralleled by Route 7 and gained more runoff water as it wound its way south, running fast and narrow until it eventually widened and dumped into Lake Lillinonah, east of Brookfield. Alongside the riverbanks near the bridge crossing, there was a reliable fishing spot, I might add. The lake was often part of our family's Sunday drive through the scenic hills and valleys, an afternoon tradition no less strong than our early dinner roast and Main Street Bake Shop rolls.

One favorite tributary of the Housatonic was Kent Falls Brook, the merged waterway consisting of a spidery network of creeks and small streams that eventually fed the wonderful Kent Falls, a park just off Route 7 between Kent and Cornwall. It was an ideal and idyllic spot for picnicking and hiking uphill next to the stepped waterfalls. The brave would even venture into the cold water in one of the collected pools. Our family enjoyed it as did many from Danbury, including the Lundy family.

Herb briefly considered taking his lunch at Kent Falls but thought the better of it, as it was a fifteen-mile diversion from his route. Frank Mark paid him to deliver milk and sell customers high-profit dairy products, not gallivant halfway to the Massachusetts border. Well, maybe he and June would take a ride to the falls on Sunday afternoon. The falls had to be running strong and the crashing water would make a wonderful thundering sound, kicking up a hazy mist.

Putting his plans aside, Herb steered the Divco east of New Milford and towards Newtown, his mind for once not on time travel, but the serenity of driving along the sparsely occupied road. He entered Newtown, taking a right onto Schoolhouse Road, stopping along the way for a couple of deliveries, then turned left on to Main Street, at the triangle where the granite war monument stood flanked by the ever-present flagpole and flag. Passing by the wonderful Yankee Drover Inn, Herb made a silent promise to himself to take June there for their next anniversary dinner and enjoy a steak so tender it could be cut with a fork.

Herb's route out of Newtown took him along Route 302, completing the last of his stops just before it reached Old Hawleyville Road near Bethel, the turning point of his other delivery route. As he approached the home of his last customer for the day, Herb pulled up under an old elm tree, not unlike the one at Rogers Park. He shut down the engine and sat there, letting the cool air envelop him through the open doors.

Herb rubbed his eyes and then sat there with them closed, wondering if he was off his rocker. He thought back to Tuesday's encounter at Veteran's Park. Could it be that he imagined the entire sequence, other than nearly hitting the man in the Ford? Could he have merely nodded off sitting in his truck at Rogers Park and simply dreamed of his time back in England during the war? It wouldn't have been the first time his mind revisited those complex and sometimes terrifying days.

But what about the trip back to the 1920s? The ghostly black pilot who fell to earth after being shot down by the Red Baron. The family, the home in South Carolina. What basis did he have to dream that?

Self-doubt began to set in. None of it made any sense, and despite June's support, she could just be humoring a man who worked hard six days a week. He did work hard; perhaps too hard. Maybe it was an extended and repeating hallucination, a flashback to the war, a trip to an imaginary cotton farm he'd read about in some magazine. Yes, that must be it – the "trip" he took through time to that farm was because of a forgotten magazine article. It had to be because it was a reasonable answer. The worldly one.

Shrugging, Herb grabbed the carrier with four milk bottles and made his last delivery of the day, started up the truck and headed for the barn, feeling better for having convinced himself the so-called time travel experience and encounter with the strange man was nothing more than a fiction of his imagination.

Chapter Twenty

"How was your day?"

"Huh? Oh, it was fine, really good. I feel much better about things."

"What things?"

"You know, the dreams I've been having about going through time, visiting places; all that nonsense."

"Sweetheart, I thought you told me they were very real experiences. The special truck and the man you met."

"I know, but I've been thinking about it, and it just makes no sense. You know I dream about the war sometimes, and I'm sure that trip to the 1920s and that black pilot had to be from some magazine article I read. I'm pretty sure I've been imagining the whole thing."

"Well, what about that manila card that came in the mail – you know when this first started? And that man?"

Herb paused. He'd forgotten about the card. "Must have been some kind of coincidence," he said, "A mistake of some sort. And as far as that man is concerned, I must have dozed off for a moment and dreamed him up." With that Herb elected to erase from his mind everything he'd imagined. It was as if a dark voice commanded him to do so, and he obeyed. But he remembered having thought about going to Kent Falls.

"Oh, I took a break along the Housatonic River today up near New Milford. It's running fast. We should really go up to Kent Falls this Sunday and have a picnic."

"That sounds nice," replied June. "I'll pack a basket for us. Maybe we can see if Stan and Rhonda want to go."

"I don't know ... Sunday's a big day at the bakeshop but maybe he can get away if we leave around two."

"I'll call Rhonda later."

"Tell her we can pick them up at the store. You know what else I thought of?"

"What?"

"I'm taking you to the Yankee Drover for our anniversary dinner. We haven't been there in ages." Herb meant to surprise June with the news but couldn't resist.

"Well mister, if you're trying to impress a girl with an expensive meal, mission accomplished," replied June, putting down her kitchen apron and wrapping her arms around Herb's neck.

Following the unexpected afternoon delight, Herb and June sat down to go through his paperwork and prepare the bills for the upcoming delivery runs. Among the stack of paper was a plain manila card. Letting out a slight "humph," Herb tossed it in the trash, ignoring the promise he'd made; a promise made in a dream, he now thought. The little dark voice spoke again and told him it was so.

June got up to call Rhonda to see if they wanted to go to Kent Falls.

June returned momentarily from the living room. She put her hand on Herb's shoulder.

"Rhonda says they can't go. Stan has a catering job on Sunday afternoon."

"Tell you what," Herb said, touching June's hand. "Let's skip church and just go in the morning before it gets too crowded, just the two of us."

Herb checked his watch. "How do you feel about a Texas Hot Weiner for dinner?" June smiled and nodded; her pot of goulash would keep for another day.

The Original Texas Hot Weiners restaurant on White Street had been a Danbury tradition for over thirty years and the memory of those small but tasty dogs was one of the things that made Herb yearn for home during his time overseas. In fact, he'd never tasted anything quite like them before or since. Having moved to a new location on West Street in 1951, the Danbury favorite was just a short drive from the Lundy home.

"The usual Mr. Lundy?" John Koukos knew many customers by name.

"Yes, for both of us," Herb replied over the protestations of his wife, who indicated that two of the dogs were more than she could eat.

"Don't worry," said Herb, nothing's going to waste," as he imagined downing perhaps two and a half or possibly three of the spicy red-hot dogs with that incredible sauce, a concoction of the inventive Miss Aphrodite.

Herb felt like he'd finally dropped a heavy pack from his shoulders, one he'd carried around for a couple of weeks. The weight and the sheer enormity of what he thought he'd been experiencing was lifted from him, and he felt relieved. He knew though, that something inside was still gnawing at him, but did not know what or why. He pushed aside the thought, taking the last bite from his own plate and with raised eyebrows, glanced over to Junc's plate. She pushed it towards him, nearly two-thirds of a hot weiner and bun left. Herb downed it in two bites and smiled. June just sighed.

Thursday. Back on the southern route with the special Magic Dairy truck, only Herb was convinced now there was nothing at all special about the truck. It was just another milk truck. Still, before heading over to Coalpit Hill Road and the nursing home where he fully intended to make a long visit with the elderly residents, he pulled over in Rogers Park near the cement pond and playground. Hopping out of the truck, he popped the hood to check on the little gold plate. It was still there. Pursing his lips, he shrugged, closed the hood, and jumped back in the truck. Putting the truck into gear, the engine died. Herb hit the starter. No go. The truck was only a few weeks old! He tried again several times, but with no luck.

Hiking up to Coalpit Hill Road, Herb knocked on the door of a nearby customer and asked to use the phone. Magic Dairy sent out another truck and called a tow truck for the one that would not start.

Within fifteen minutes, Harry Stevens arrived with a different truck, put it back to back with Herb's and they unloaded the remaining milk bottles and assorted dairy products plus the ice bags into the replacement truck. On a hunch, Harry tried to start Herb's truck and it fired up immediately. He looked at Herb.

"I thought you said this was dead as a doornail."

"It was. I tried again and again, and it wouldn't start."

"Maybe you flooded the carburetor," Harry ventured.

"Maybe."

"I'll catch the tow truck on the way out," and with that, Harry drove the special Magic Dairy truck away, leaving Herb to his thoughts. Nothing more than a coincidence, Herb decided, and Harry was probably right about flooding the carburetor. He headed over towards Bethel to complete his route, stopping at the home on Putnam Drive with the new owners to convince them to sign up with Magic Dairy. They agreed.

"Herb! Hey, there he is!" The cries of welcome greeted Herb as he walked into the nursing home, feeling like a celebrity simply for taking a few moments to call upon these old folks who had so few visitors.

"What did you bring us?"

"Well, we've got a whole crate of milk and today I brought some cottage cheese too if that's OK," Herb looked at the nurse who smiled and nodded. It was always an easy sell.

Herb made small talk with a few of the residents including a normally gruff man who constantly wore his World War I campaign hat but lit up every time he saw Herb. The grizzled veteran looked like a wrinkled drill instructor in the darned hat, but it was one of the only sources of joy and pride for the dying man, and everyone let him be. Two old festering and inoperable war wounds were overcoming him although he was only in his late fifties, and Herb knew his remaining time on the planet was short, so he spent a few extra minutes with this brave hero on every visit. Today for the first time, he wondered what compelled him to do so.

Chapter Twenty-One

The Sunday morning roads were nearly empty, most people either sleeping in or attending the church of their choice. There was a slight chill in the air, but spring was making headway towards summer. Only a few spots on the road still shone with running water from the last of the melting ice, running down from nearby hills, and a dusting of road sand lined the edges, the final reminder of the plows and sanding trucks that not long before had kept Route 7 open to traffic during months of winter snows.

Creatures of habit, most people who attend a church or even a regular meeting of some sort choose the same seats again and again. Thus, when the Lundy's failed to occupy the front pew at the First Congregational Church on Sunday morning, Reverend Waller scanned the sanctuary thinking they may have taken different seats while doubting it all along. Not finding them, he proceeded with his sermon, a carefully written and re-written story about how impossible it was for a rich man to get to heaven. By design or coincidence, with the money sermon fresh in everyone's mind, the large, silver-clad collection plates were passed by the ushers, as the very public offering took place, with some nosy types spying to see the amount of the previous giver's offering.

It was my first week to sit in the impressive sanctuary of the church for the entire service as a "member," having finally gotten my confirmation and my very own Bible, embossed on the front cover with my full name, in gold lettering. It was a King James Bible with "helps" they called it, meaning colorful illustrations and side notes. I took the carefully printed folded flyer that told us what hymns would be sung, the subject of the sermon, and so on, and sat on the inside seat where I could see past the large hat of the lady in front of us. I could see the pulpit, the flailing arms of the organist and the choir in their robes. What I did not see was Mr. and Mrs. Lundy, though I thought little of it.

Herb and June Lundy drove with windows partly open, to capture the crisp morning air on their drive to Kent Falls. A woven basket contained the carefully prepared lunch and June brought a blanket to sit on and a thermos of coffee. The Housatonic River was rushing alongside the road, veering closer at some points, and nearly out of sight at others. Before long, Herb steered into the nearly empty dirt parking lot and shut off the motor. They had Kent Falls almost all to themselves.

Wearing jackets against the cool morning, Herb and June hiked over to the base of the falls, alongside the stream that led to the Housatonic. A canopy of tall trees framed the stepped trail alongside waterfalls as sprays of falling water created a mist that cast a vapory shroud over the crude walkway comprised of steps made from wide logs that led to the top.

The large logs embedded along the path served to help ambitious hikers scale the steep hill and separated by only a few feet in some places from the roaring water, the logs were in some places slick from the sprayed mist.

"Be careful along here, June." Herb walked behind her, chivalrously aiming to catch her if she fell or slipped. Barely reaching the second collection pool, Herb spotted something moving in the woods and as he turned to get a better look, his foot slipped on one of the slick logs and down he went, his head snapping back, and then striking a log further down. His head spun, he saw stars and was out cold.

"Oh, no! NO!" June screamed for help. A man and his teenage son, hiking down from the top were there in a moment, the son checking on Herb while the man tried to comfort a nearly hysterical June.

Coming to her senses quickly, June dipped her scarf into the pool and dabbed Herb's face with the icy water. After a minute, Herb slowly opened his eyes and the world around him spun. He closed them again.

"He's awake," the boy calmly announced. "Help him sit up."

A large lump was already forming near Herb's left temple. Another inch or so to the right and he might have had more serious problems.

"Honey, are you OK?" June was calmer now that Herb came around.

"Ish fell." Herb babbled a mumbled response and looked up, seeing several people he did not recognize.

"Let's get him down the hill," said the man as he and his son each took one of Herb's arms over and behind their neck and stumbled unevenly down the hill. It took a few minutes to navigate the log steps.

"I'd take him to the hospital, ma'am," advised the man. "He may have a concussion or maybe even worse."

June agreed and fished the car key from Herb's jacket. She ran over to the car to bring it closer while the man and his son helped Herb stagger to the edge of the parking area.

Herb seemed to be coming around, other than the swelling near his temple. June decided to bypass the nearby New Milford Hospital and took him directly to Danbury Hospital to be closer to home. She hoped the extra travel time would not make a difference in his treatment, and besides, she knew the admitting nurse, Sandra Hope, who would be working today.

Driving swiftly but safely, June navigated down Route 7 as it became Route 202 and followed Federal Road into town, connecting to White Street and then turning right onto Locust Avenue coming to a halt outside the emergency room entrance at the hospital. Herb walked in unsteadily with June holding his arm, with a throbbing headache and an impressive looking bump that was obvious to nurse Sandra.

There was only one other patient waiting and it sounded like someone with the flu. Sandra briefly took some information and guided Herb inside for treatment. Herb turned to thank her for her kindness, and everything went white as he collapsed to the linoleum floor.

Chapter Twenty-Two

Herb felt a slight stinging sensation in his arm. It was an IV needle connected to a hanging bag of saline solution dripping into his vein to keep him hydrated. The window near his bed indicated it was nighttime. The clothes he wore earlier were gone, replaced by a flimsy hospital gown. He tried to remember what happened and why he was apparently in the hospital but could not. His eyes tried to focus on a man standing at the foot of his bed.

Mostly disguised by the lab coat, eyeglasses, and stethoscope around his neck, the doctor with the long hair looked at Herb with concern.

"You've had quite a fall, Mr. Lundy."

Herb tried to talk but his throat was dry.

"That's OK, don't talk. You've had a rather serious concussion and when you fell here in the hospital, you bruised your wrist, but it's not too bad, fortunately, and you'll heal up just fine."

Herb lamely looked over at his right arm. Indeed, his lower forearm down to his hand looked bruised with a splotchy purple color. There was a steady dull pain. He looked back at the doctor, this time with a quizzical expression that slowly transformed into awareness.

The doctor glanced behind him then leaned closer to Herb and spoke. "Yes Herb, it is I. You seem to have forgotten our arrangement and misplaced your promise."

Herb stammered a few unintelligible words. The worst of it was he thought for sure he was hallucinating from his head injury. He was sure of it. He closed and then reopened his eyes. The same man was still there.

"Herb, do you know the parable of the mustard seed?"

Herb nodded his head and mouthed, "Yes." He knew it well. Reverend Waller talked about it often enough. Someone with faith as small as a mustard seed could command a mountain to move, and it would move. Nothing was impossible.

"You're not hallucinating, Herb. My being here is quite real, just as it was in the park and the other day when you stopped for coffee."

Herb noticed that there was no noise or obvious activity in the hospital. There was always something going on in a hospital. Nurses running around, noises from the nurse station, people calling out for help.

Herb felt confused and ashamed at the same time. His faith had been tested and he had failed miserably. His faith was not even as large as a tiny mustard seed. He genuinely looked and felt sorry.

"Give it another chance, Herb. Give *me* another chance." With that, he touched Herb on his bruised wrist and the pain immediately subsided. He then touched the lump on Herb's temple. Herb's grogginess disappeared in an instant. He had mental clarity. Herb looked into the kind eyes of his visitor and smiled, tears forming in his own eyes. At that moment, he realized the other voice he'd heard encouraging him to distrust his experiences was from a darker place, disguised as one of reason, of the world.

"I will," Herb said in a croaky voice. "I will."

A breeze suddenly picked up outside and Herb heard a tree outside his window rustle forcefully in the wind. When he looked back, the visitor was gone. He heard a doctor scurrying down the hallway. A phone rang at the nurse's station. Herb looked over at his suddenly healed wrist. Underneath his wrist lay a small plain manila card.

June stopped in again to check on her husband and found him to be awake and in a fine spirit.

"Sweetheart, how are you feeling? She sat in the leather chair next to the bed. "I've just had something to eat."

"Feeling much better, I must say," Herb replied, holding up his wrist as evidence. It was no longer swollen and most of the ugly color was gone. Herb shook his wrist back and forth. June sat back in the chair, her eyes dancing between Herb's wrist and face.

"Why that's wonderful! What about your head?" She gently touched his temple, being careful not to press too hard. The gauze wrapping was a bit loose.

"It's much better, too. I could go home right now."

"Not so fast, mister. The doctor said they're keeping you overnight so just settle that in your mind. I've already told Mr. Mark what happened, and he said to take as much time as you need."

Herb thought about missing work tomorrow. Monday. It was his day to drive the special truck. Oh well. His adventure would just have to wait a few days to resume. He reached for June's hand and held it, then closed his eyes. He whispered a barely perceptible prayer.

"Father, thank you for your grace and your healing powers. Thank you for the good doctors and nurses here who serve so many in need. Thank you for my good wife, my home and my job. Thank you for the food you place on our table, and most of all Father, thank you for the opportunity to grow closer to your Word. Amen." He released June's hand.

June was a little stunned by her husband's prayer. He did not often publicly display a show a faith outside of church, even to her. A man who a few days ago had explained away his time trip of faith and even skipped church was suddenly praying out loud in a hospital.

Something had happened while she was away at dinner. Something very mysterious, but very real.

Kent Falls State Park
Wikimedia Commons - Jllm06

Chapter Twenty-Three

"The fruit of the Spirit is patience..."

Tuesday morning arrived with constant
rain, the kind that lasts all day; not a driving rain
by any means but more of a hard drizzle, soaking
the ground for the thirsty tulip and crocus bulbs.
It mattered not. Herb had called Mr. Mark
yesterday afternoon after getting home from the
hospital and assured him he'd be back at work
the next day. Herb's wrist was perfectly fine to
drive, and the only remaining sign that he'd
fallen and hit his head was a faint red spot the
size of a quarter near his temple. Herb was alert
and aware. The doctor at Danbury Hospital was
impressed with his speedy recovery; confused if
the truth is told, but regardless, he gladly let the
milkman go home with his blessings. All the
same, Mr. Mark insisted Herb take the new Divco
to make Herb's day as easy as possible.

The cold rain felt good on Herb's face.
Rather than see it as a nuisance, today he
regarded it as nature's replenishment. A gift,
really. May flowers and all that. Besides, his
Magic Dairy slicker would keep him dry while he
ran his western route. Just in case something
unusual came up, Herb tucked the small manila
card from the hospital in his pants pocket,

thinking for a moment he'd swing by Rogers Park but forgetting about it as the day wore on.

The Divco had just had its first oil change service and was running well. After an uneventful route that took a bit longer than usual due to the rain and rain-impaired drivers, Herb swung over to Deer Hill Avenue to make a stop at nearby 98 Garfield Avenue to fulfill a special request. Oddly enough, the order was in a brown sack that had been given to him stapled shut. Why they couldn't wait until Thursday when Herb would be on his regular run was not even a question. With competition from several other dairies, the customer was always right, at least in the eyes and mind of Frank Mark. Herb, too.

Herb guided the Divco up Deer Hill Avenue from the north, turning right on West Wooster Street and then making an immediate left onto Garfield Avenue. Just a few houses in, the stunning Garfield Elm tree commanded the street, overseeing every car or pedestrian as it towered over the home at number 98 as well as the entire roadway.

"Ah yes," Herb said to himself. "The famous Garfield Elm, some three hundred years old so they say." What a stately and impressive tree it was, and lucky too, to have avoided elm disease that had rid the city of so many other of its kind. The rotund trunk intruded into the roadway, or as some might say, the roadway intruded into the elm's space. Its massive roots upended pavement and sidewalk making routine maintenance by the city street maintenance crew a necessary if not ultimately futile task as the concrete and asphalt quilt of patches would attest. It could be argued that the tree and its roots presented a driving and walking hazard, but since it had been there since the 1600s, no one had yet summoned the courage to venture a plan to have it removed.

Herb pulled up under the elm in front of number 98, instinctively turning the tires to the curb even though he was not parked on a hill. By now, the rain had stopped completely. He reached back for the special order but instead, pulled back and sat down on the driver's seat, contemplating a random thought he could not quite process. For a reason unknown to him at that moment, like a pitcher who shakes off the catcher's curveball sign and chooses to throw a fastball instead, Herb reached into his pants pocket and touched the manila card he had gotten at the hospital.

Now, in all my formative years growing up in Danbury, and living just a few blocks away from Garfield Avenue, I had never found a reason to visit that street or the huge elm. The places I traveled were predicated mostly on where my friends lived and where we went fishing. Frankly, the bulk of my activities as a kid were hosted by Rogers Park whether it was on one of the baseball diamonds, the long open field we used for football, playing tennis, or even hitting golf balls on the miniature chip-and-putt course in the shady grove of trees next to the tennis courts.

At Rogers Park, we kids would reliably find the Good Humor man on his three-wheeled motorcycle with the ice cream cooler mounted on the back, or we'd frequent the shallow cement pool, its seams marked with black tar stripes and its cruel rough surface the source of many a bloody scrape. The memorial rose trellises held only minor interest to us kids, but inside the brick War Memorial building, we could bowl duckpins or attend a school dance or battle of the bands. So, in the overall view and history of growing up on the south side of Danbury, Rogers Park and the corner pharmacy with its fountain cherry Cokes and packs of baseball cards held all our interest where a three-hundred-year-old tree gained none.

Unexpectedly but not surprisingly, Herb's world went white as his finger touched the manila card. In that vaporous instant, he didn't have the opportunity to wonder why the card worked at this elm tree as well as the one in Rogers Park; he just knew another experience was about to unfold.

Opening his eyes, Herb was still parked

under the Garfield Elm, but it seemed just a bit bigger, and the cars along the curb were different. They looked like the ones he'd seen in Popular Mechanics magazine, the article about cars of the future. The driveway at 98 Garfield Avenue was heaved up from the elm tree roots to nearly make parking difficult. Walking on that side of the street was to risk turning an ankle. Herb stretched his shoulders and shook his head back and forth. His eyes focused on the license plate of the car parked in front of him. Instead of the dark blue field with white numbers and the word "CONNECTICUT" imprinted along the bottom, the plate he saw was a lighter shade of blue fading to white, with "Connecticut" spelling out demurely along the top edge and "Constitution State" along the bottom. The license number itself was dark blue instead of white and in the upper right-hand corner was a date sticker: FEB 2005.

Herb glanced at a few other cars on the street. They all had this new plate with the gradient blue to white effect. Stapled to the tree was a handmade note saying, "SAVE THE GARFIELD ELM" with a phone number. Why was the "203" area code included in front of the number? No one needed to dial 203 locally. It didn't make sense.

"Where'd you get the old Magic Dairy truck?" A man startled Herb with his unlikely question.

"Excuse me?" Herb looked over at the man, somewhat portly and obviously in his fifties or so. He carried but did not use a cane.

"I said, where'd you get that old Magic Dairy truck? Is Marcus Dairy doing some kind of nostalgia thing?"

"Well ... no," replied Herb, "This is a Magic Dairy truck, not Marcus Dairy."

"Well, I can see that ya danged fool. I thought maybe Marcus was doing some kind of special promotion with its old trucks, you know, from the takeover."

"What takeover is that?" Herb was totally confused, and the man was becoming exasperated.

"You know, back in what was it, 1987 I guess when Marcus bought out that Frank Mark guy after his wife passed."

Herb was jolted into the moment, realizing he was no longer in 1957, but probably 2004. It was warm enough and leaves on the maple trees were turning, so if the FEB 2005 license plate was still good, then he'd be in September maybe, or maybe early October of 2004.

"Uh, yeah." Herb turned to the gentleman on the street. "Yeah, it is indeed a very well-preserved Magic Dairy truck. In fact, it runs like new, and they even gave me this old uniform to look the part." He was playing along at the moment.

"Not a lot of people still get milk delivered," said the man. He peeked inside the truck. "Wow, they even give you the old bottles. I remember them from when I was a kid."

A strange sound came from the man's pocket, kind of an alarm, or was it a musical jingle? Herb thought the man was carrying a transistor radio. The man reached into his pocket and pulled out what looked kind of like a transistor radio, but it was super thin. And there was a bright image on the front of it. Odd.

"Excuse me," said the man. I've gotta take this." He held the transistor radio up to his head like a telephone and began walking away and for some reason, talking into his radio.

"Take what?" Herb called out but to no avail. What do you "take" from a transistor radio unless it's a song on WLAD or WINE?

The man turned and called out, "Nice old truck, buddy! See ya around!" Herb waved weakly. He slowly realized that he was nearly fifty years into the future. His hands were not wrinkled nor covered with brown spots. He checked the mirror and saw the same face he'd seen this morning. Well, now.

Herb sat a moment and thought. He had a special order for 98 Garfield Avenue. He was parked in front of 98 Garfield Avenue. Even though he was forty-seven years late, Herb decided he must have been sent here to fill the order and stepped out of the truck, gingerly avoiding the massive roots of the elm. The homes on Garfield Avenue did not look substantially different from the last time he was here, back in 1957, or last week, in fact. A few homes had what looked to be metal siding instead of clapboards. There was a tiny little blue car with a round logo he'd never seen and the word, PRIUS in chrome letters. It seemed to have a short radio antenna coming out of its roof. Herb's confusion grew along with his wonder. He knocked firmly on the front door of 98 Garfield Avenue.

Momentarily, an older woman, perhaps in her sixties, opened the door. She wore not the typical flowery house dress and supportive shoes Herb was used to seeing on a female of that vintage, but a colorful knit wrap and rather tight dungarees like kids wore plus a model of Keds sneakers Herb had never seen before. They were pink and white and had a rounded checkmark on the side. The lady smiled warmly at Herb.

"Mrs. Oulette?" Herb read the name written on the brown sack. He hadn't delivered to this address before, so the customer name was not familiar to him.

"Why, yes. You must be Mr. Lundy. I've been waiting for you." She turned and walked into the house, waving him to follow behind. Mrs. Oulette stopped on the porch and half-turned towards Herb. Continuing her thought:

"For quite some time."

Herb passed through the front door and glanced around the room. It looked normal to him except for a large, flat screen of some sort mounted on a wall. A portable radio in the kitchen played soft music that was completely unfamiliar to the visitor.

"Uh, how long have you been waiting?" Herb thought he knew the answer.

"Oh, only forty-seven years or so. You're late!" The lady smiled again, revealing gleaming white teeth and exuding a serenity with which Herb had only a fleeting acquaintance. He felt like the subject of an experiment, or perhaps a supernatural joke. He decided to go with it.

"Have you lived here long?" Herb decided to try some small talk.

"Yes," came the reply, not answering Herb's real question. Then she explained. "I grew up here. Before my parents passed, they signed the house over to me, and I've continued to live here even though I didn't really want to."

"Why is that?" Herb sat at the kitchen table as his host gestured to him, pointing at a chair. Now he was intrigued.

"I graduated from Danbury High School in 1957. Did well, top ten percent of the class. I applied to a few colleges even though my parents could not afford to send me, but the registrar from a small college in Vermont called the house to inform me not only had I been accepted but that they were offering a full scholarship. Only I didn't know that."

"How come? What happened?"

"As it turns out, I wasn't home when the call came. I was up at Candlewood Lake with a few friends. My mother took the call, and apparently politely thanked them but told them I was too young to go away to school."

"That's awful!" Herb was shocked but not totally surprised that parents were reluctant to let their young daughter attend school out of town. "What did you do?"

"Well, I didn't know anything about it, and I ended up at WestConn, but back then it was known as Danbury State Teacher's College. I didn't want to be a teacher but that's what a lot of girls were doing, and so I went along."

Herb had never heard the term, "WestConn" but he had heard of course, of Danbury State so he went along, assuming the name had changed somewhere along the way.

"So, I went to Danbury State, got my degree and became a teacher. Good one, too. Earned my masters a few years later and worked my way up to assistant principal at Rogers Park Middle School as the years went by."

"Wait. Rogers Park Middle School?" There was no school in Rogers Park. "Do you mean a junior high?

"Well, we called it a junior high when I was a kid but yes, middle school." Herb sat back. Where in the park would they put a "middle school?"

"So, you did okay for yourself, it sounds like. Am I right?" Herb was being encouraging.

Barbara Oulette leaned forward and looked Herb in the eye. "Yes, I did okay," she uttered the words slowly, "But I didn't do what I wanted."

"Which was?"

"Mr. Lundy, I've always wanted to be an artist. The serious kind. The kind whose paintings are hung in galleries, sold at auctions, the kind whose name is mentioned with respect at shows while guests sip their pretentious glasses of wine." She waved her hand towards the hallway. "You see?"

Herb stood and stepped towards the wide hallway leading to a dining room. On its walls were hung more than a dozen skillfully crafted landscapes and portraits. The artist obviously had talent and knew how to use shadow and color, but they weren't spectacular. He looked knowingly over to Mrs. Oulette. She'd suffered a long time bravely enduring a career for which she did not care. The pain of putting on a happy face for the sake of others. He wondered how he would deal with such a fate. Herb loved his job and the freedom of choosing how his day would pan out, how much extra income he could make purely based on his own personality and salesmanship. He was perhaps an artist in his own way, creating a new painting each day from canvases and oil colors that did not change.

"Yes, they're mine. I have more in the basement. I think they're good. In fact, I know they're good but they're not great. I just never was able to get that kind of training. And so, I've been waiting. For you."

"For me? Why for me?" Herb eyed the brown sack. Now that he thought of it, the sack was not at all heavy, like it would be if it contained cream or some other dairy product. He walked slowly back towards the table. He looked at the sack, then looked at Mrs. Oulette. She raised her eyebrows a bit, nodding her head to one side. Herb pushed the sack towards her. She carefully pulled back the stapled folds and reached inside.

Barbara Oulette sat back in her chair while Herb, in wonder, slowly lowered himself to his, both hands on the table supporting his slow descent. He took off his Magic Dairy hat and leaned forward, expectantly. The woman removed a large folder with a silver graphic on the cover. There was an imprinted logo for Bennington College adorning the cover. It was a very plain logo, not like the decorative round seals with which Herb was familiar. Mrs. Oulette opened the folder, read the document inside for a moment, then pursed her lips and began to quietly sob, just a bit. Herb stood to his feet to comfort the woman. He glanced at the yellowed letter. It was a brief typewritten form addressed to Miss Barbara Oulette, 98 Garfield Avenue, Danbury, Conn.

Dear Miss Oulette;

It is our pleasure to inform you that you have been accepted for admission to Bennington College in the Visual Arts program. In deference to your young age, we appreciate that you may wish to matriculate at a time later than 1957.

If that is the case, you may view this letter and the accompanying documents to be valid indefinitely. One of our benefactors has provided a trust account with scholarship funds for promising art students such as yourself and therefore, your tuition fees will be waived, regardless of when you begin classes. We look forward to welcoming you to the Bennington family.

Warmest Regards,

Herb was as stunned as Mrs. Oulette. "Regardless of when you begin classes," he slowly repeated the words in the letter. He thought to himself that the school didn't expect "indefinitely" to be nearly a half-century.

"I'm going to Bennington. I'm going to BENNINGTON!" Mrs. Oulette leaped to her feet and hugged Herb around the neck. "I don't know why, Mr. Lundy, but I know that it was placed in my heart to wait. To patiently wait for my turn, even if decades passed. I knew it in my heart."

Herb turned his head slightly. "By the way, how do you know my name?"

"I don't know. In my dreams, I often heard the name, Lundy and never knew why until today. When I referred to you as Mr. Lundy and you didn't correct me, I knew why."

"How can you be sure this letter is still valid?" Even promises made by institutions of higher learning must have some limits, Herb thought.

"I'm going to call them!" Mrs. Oulette reached for one of those thin transistor radios that had a small luminous screen and buttons on the front. "I even have their number on my contact list. My neighbor's son went there."

Son? Herb thought Bennington was a women's college. Things change. Mrs. Oulette pressed a few buttons and held the device up to her ear, as the man in the street had done.

"Registrar's office, please." Herb looked on with no small amount of wonder as the woman talked into a little black rectangle that had no cord attached to it. The conversation went on while Herb studied some of the paintings.

Pressing another button, Mrs. Oulette put down her ... phone. "They said it's valid. The trust was funded for one hundred years. I can start anytime I want. It's just amazing. Thank you, Mr. Lundy. Thank you. You have no idea how much this means to me."

Herb thought he did but decided it was time to leave before Mrs. Oulette started asking questions; about him, about his milk truck. She walked him to the door.

"I've got so much to do. Maybe I'll sell the house. Oh, I just don't know. I'd miss that big old tree out front." She pulled on Herb's sleeve and stopped him as they reached the door. She looked out at the old truck. For the first time, she noticed his old fashioned outfit. "Mr. Lundy, whatever dream it is you're waiting for, no matter how long it takes, be patient." She held up the letter to make her point. The serene and confident look on her face told Herb what he needed to know, but she said it anyway. "It's worth the wait." She smiled, looking out the door window and whispered to the room. "His will be done."

Mrs. Oulette bade Herb goodbye and closed the door, busily coming to grips with her lifetime dream, finally come to pass. Herb sighed deeply and stepped back towards his truck, avoiding the roots of the ancient elm. For a moment, Herb thought about driving around town to see what it looked like a half-century into the future, and since it seemed to be early fall, perhaps even heading over towards the fairgrounds to see if it was open. It was not to be. He stepped up into the little Divco and into the white light.

Opening his eyes, Herb noticed the Magic Dairy truck was idling, still parked in front of 98 Garfield Avenue but things were different again. A brand new 1957 Chevy Biscayne with the tail fins and a two-tone paint job was parked in front of him. A dark blue CONNECTICUT license plate was encased in a chrome frame and a Dan-Ridge emblem was affixed to the trunk lid. The sack for delivery to 98 Garfield Avenue was gone. Looking up, he saw a young girl, about seventeen, looking at him through the front window of the house. Sighing heavily, Herb put the Divco truck in gear and pulled out to head back to the dairy.

Just before 2 p.m. Herb steered the Divco onto the gravel drive at Magic Dairy and chugged to a stop. He pondered what had just happened or was it what he'd just imagined. He sighed deeply and rubbed his hands across his face.

"You alright, Herb?" Harry's voice startled Herb and he jumped sideways. "Whoa! OK, I guess you're still with us." What was Harry doing here at this hour?

"Harry, why are you here so late ... again?" Herb had a quizzical look to him as he stepped down from the truck.

"Oh, just helping unload. Mr. Mark asked me to hang around for a while." Harry didn't like to fib, but a fib was called for. He changed the subject. "Hey, did the lady on Garfield Avenue like her delivery?" Herb indicated that she was quite pleased but said nothing more of it.

"New guy?" Herb looked across the lot to a man unloading a Divco. He had long hair, but it was tucked under a Magic Dairy ball cap.

"Yeah, he comes around occasionally, kind of a part-timer I guess you could say. Good guy. Hard worker."

With that, the man stood up from his work and turned fully towards Herb. He was about thirty-five feet away. Sunlight streamed through the newly bloomed leaves of a nearby maple tree, highlighting the man's confident and serene face. Herb's mouth fell open and he looked questioningly at Harry for a long moment, then back over to the other truck. The man was gone.

Harry just shrugged. "He comes and goes when he wants. And by the way, he's the one who gave me that sack for delivery to 98 Garfield Avenue. Said it was a special order."

Chapter Twenty-Four

"Stan called. He and Rhonda want to get together for dinner." June greeted Herb with the news. It had been a few months since the couples had really spent any time with each other. In fact, June and Rhonda saw each other more than Herb did Stan, both belonging to a local sewing club. Otherwise, both families were just so busy and with Herb and Stan both getting up so early six days a week, it was a challenge to agree on arrangements.

"Oh uh, that's a great idea." Herb hung up his Magic Dairy jacket and cap and absently reached over to receive June's kiss on his cheek. "We can make it on Saturday, can't' we? Since I don't have to get up early on Sunday?"

"That's what Rhonda said, too. She said Stan can have Michael open the store on Sunday. I told her we ought to go to the Old Oak. Haven't been there in ages."

Herb really liked the Old Oak. The brick facade, the large porthole windows. It was something of an institution, offering some of the best Italian food in the area. It was a charming and intimate venue for good friends to meet and dine. He was up for it. He also wanted to get Stan aside for a few minutes and have him do a sanity check for his old friend. Herb didn't want to have doubts, but at the same time, he couldn't help himself.

Herb's route on Thursday proved uneventful and when he swung by the elm tree in Rogers Park, there was no manila card. He even looked around on the ground for one before leaving. It made sense in light of his recent adventure on Garfield Avenue he thought, to skip a day every so often.

A couple of days passed, and Herb finished up Saturday's route in near-record time, missing his best-ever by just two minutes, then wheeled his Divco back to the shop before heading home to shower and dress for dinner.

Promptly at 6:30 p.m., Herb and June pulled up to Stan and Rhonda's home out past Federal Highway. It was a three-bedroom ranch style home built into the side of a hill with a basement that Stan couldn't quite keep dry, at least in the April rains combined with snowmelt. Truth be told, his pump was by far not the only sump pump to find purpose in a basement in Western Connecticut in the late 1950s.

Riding over to the Old Oak on Liberty Street just off Main Street, Rhonda and June did most of the talking in the back seat while Stan and Herb were mostly silent, occasionally muttering a comment and pointing out something of interest along the way during the

10-minute drive. Herb guided the four-door Ford Customline west along White Street, past the big Leahy gas ball and Meeker's hardware store. After making a left at Main Street and passing the Empress and Palace movie theaters, Herb took the next left on Keeler Street bearing right on Liberty Street to the corner of Town Hill Avenue. He made a mental note of the marquees outside the two theaters. The Empress was featuring *The Incredible Shrinking Man* while the Palace was showing a double feature with *Abbot and Costello Meet the Invisible Man*, plus Jeff Chandler starring in *Man in the Shadow*. Herb assumed that none of those three movies would appeal to June as he turned into a small gravel parking lot across from the Old Oak.

Thinking that he'd not get a chance to talk privately with Stan once inside the restaurant, Herb suggested to the still-chatting June and Rhonda to go and get a table. He and Stan would both take a draft beer if the drink order was requested before they joined the wives. He motioned to Stan and they both leaned on the Ford, Stan drawing on a cigarette and toeing the gravel.

"Something you want to say?"

"Yeah, I guess. Look, Stan, you've known me forever. Did you ever think I'd go off my rocker?"

"Not for a moment, Herb. You're as steady

as an oak," motioning his head towards the restaurant.

"Alright, look. I've been having these uh, episodes at work, a couple of times a week now for the last few weeks where I know it sounds ridiculous, I get to time travel, and it's always something that has to do with emotions or learning a lesson or actually, I'm not quite sure."

"Time travel, huh? How many times have you read that H.G. Wells book now?"

"I know, that's what I was thinking, that this time travel stuff is planted in my head from that book and maybe I'm dozing off and dreaming. I don't know. It all seems real enough when it happens."

"I'm not going to judge you, Herb. I'm not going to call you crazy, but I am a little worried."

"I know. I'm worried, too."

"Have you told June?"

"Yes, yes I have, and she's been supportive, but I don't know if she thinks I'm nuts or is just humoring me, or what." He thought for a moment and then said convincingly, "I think she believes me."

"So, what started all this?" Stan was playing along, even though June had told Rhonda, and Rhonda, of course, had confided in Stan, swearing him to secrecy.

"Well, I know it may sound crazy, but I think I met Jesus. Down at Rogers Park, and I saw him again over in Ridgefield, once more when I hit my head, then again for just a second back at Magic Dairy." Silence. Stan shuffled his shoe in the gravel again, stomping out his cigarette. He exhaled slowly and looked over at his friend.

"I accept what you're saying, Herb. I do. Because why not? You're a believer, aren't you? So am I. He can do whatever He wants, and time means nothing. Everything we're told relates to eternity. If there is an eternity, then there is no time, am I right? Or not time in the way we think of it."

Herb was relieved and he showed it by stretching his neck back, looking to the deepening blue sky. Stan did, however, challenge Herb wanting to know how the events took place.

"He told me that the new Divco truck I was driving had a special power. He told me to look for a manila card like the ones you might find in the card catalog at the library. He said it would be tucked into the corner branch of the big elm tree by the pond at Rogers Park. When I took that card and stepped back into the truck, I'd be transported to someplace in my subconscious."

"So that's how you were able to time travel?"

"Yes. I touch the card in my truck, and I'm gone."

Stan sighed heavily. He did not think Herb

was losing it, but he was very confused.

"Herb, exactly what were those emotions or lessons you mentioned?"

"Well, let me see." Herb rolled his eyes up, thinking. "The first time I was back in the war on a mission and some German pilot was coming right at us, but he didn't fire. So, I didn't fire, either."

"And how did that make you feel?"

"Well, I know it sounds stupid, but when we got back to do the debriefing, I just felt like this guy probably didn't fire because his guns jammed and I could have shot him straight on, but for some reason, I didn't. It was weird because everyone was still just like they were in 1944 and it really hit me how much I miss those guys. And then I thought about that German pilot and how I guess I let him live, at least for another day. I felt close to him like we were fellow travelers on some horrible, awful trip. Stan, I felt love for the man. I did."

"Then what?"

"Well, not long after that trip, I found myself back in the twenties, I think at some farm. It was kind of a poor farm, but these folks weren't at all concerned with how much money they had or didn't have. They had a very close-knit family and a love for the Lord. It was obvious. It didn't matter that they were poor, they had, I don't know ... absolute joy."

"Interesting. Is there more?"

"Yes, the next week, I was in Ridgefield and met up again with the man I think is Jesus. I didn't really travel through time, but time did stop. I mean nothing around us moved while he was there, so maybe that was time travel. Anyway, we had kind of a deep conversation about things like the love of money being the root of all evil and being poor in spirit but rich in the blessings of God. That kind of stuff."

"How did that make you feel?" Stan was expertly playing the role of counselor.

"Well," Herb thought a moment. "Peaceful, I guess. At ease. Not worried about the normal stuff any longer."

Stan thought a moment. "Herb my friend, you know what love, joy, and peace are?"

Herb drew a blank.

"It's in the Bible, Herb. The fruit of the Spirit, or at least that's a few of them. Might want to look that up. I think it's Galatians five-something."

Stan clapped his old friend on the back. "Let's go inside before they think we've abandoned them." The two walked over to the door under the awning. Stan grabbed the door handle and paused, looking at Herb. "You don't have one of those manila cards on you, do you?"

Chapter Twenty-Five

Herb and June were back in church the next Sunday, in the front pew as usual under the approving nod of Reverend Waller. Herb felt like he was growing, learning, but that there was more to come. After talking with Stan before dinner at the Old Oak, Herb had pulled out the Bible shortly after he got home and scanned for the "fruit of the Spirit." He found it in Galatians 5:22-23.

22 *But the fruit of the Spirit is love, joy, peace, patience, kindness, goodness, faithfulness,* 23 *gentleness, and self-control. Against such things, there is no law.*

Herb thought about the fruit while falling asleep after Saturday's big dinner. It was all starting to make sense, thanks to Stan's friendship and patience. Herb didn't know why, but he was being given the gift of grace through personal experiences of the teachings of Paul the Apostle. It was nearly beyond comprehension.

Other thoughts soon crowded them out. Bedtime on Saturday came later than normal – ten-thirty, and as thoughts of the fruit faded, he dreamed of flying in his Divco truck, looking down on the grasslands and farms below, the unevenly shaped plots bordered by stone and wood fences. As he marveled at the scene beneath him, one with which he was painfully and intimately familiar resulting from thirty-five missions over Europe, a loud repeating machine sound shocked him from his peaceful reverie. Still dreaming, he looked out the side window of his Divco truck to see an oncoming Messerschmidt ME-109, machine guns and cannons blazing, cutting his truck to shreds. He was falling now, the fields growing larger as he lost awareness.

Herb looked up. The choir and congregation were singing the benediction. "Praise God from whom all blessings flow…" He had somehow missed the sermon, the hymns, the offering; or if he hadn't missed them, he didn't remember. June nudged him and they stood together, exiting the pew, merging with other churchgoers shuffling back and forth towards the doors. Stepping into the sunlight, Herb led June straight to their car, not stopping to speak with Reverend Waller and barely nodding to his friends and neighbors who tried to catch his eye.

"What is it? What's wrong?" June demanded as Herb scattered gravel leaving the church parking lot.

"Nothing. It's nothing." Herb was insistent but strangely abrupt. He cut in front of a car heading south on Deer Hill Avenue, then turned sharply left onto West Street as the light changed to red.

"Herb, slow down!" June tugged on his jacket sleeve.

Catching himself, Herb eased off the gas and looked at June with a strange expression, one that reflected a confused and lost boy. It was a look June had never seen on Herb's face, not in his darkest moments. Sighing deeply, Herb gathered himself and steered the Customline carefully under the low-clearance railroad bridge that had trapped many an unaware trucker, and up Lake Avenue past the El Dorado, turning left onto Merrimac then finally to Victor Street and home. Herb killed the engine and set the parking brake. Quiet now, he sat still with a dazed look, looking out the windshield but not seeing anything. June thought about trying to snap him out of whatever moment he was in but thought better of it and quietly went inside to finish preparing the Sunday meal.

After a few moments, Herb stepped out of the Ford but didn't go inside. Instead, he walked back to the corner of Merrimac and on up a block to Lake Avenue. He stood there at the corner expressionless, watching cars go by, pondering what to do. A car horn snapped him out of his dreamlike state. It was Harry. Spying Herb, he turned off Lake Avenue and pulled over. Herb walked over to the passenger window.

"You lost there, Herb?" Harry wore his ever-present smile.

"Ah, just out for a bit of walk, enjoying the fresh air."

"Are you now?" Harry seemed skeptical. His smile faded as he put on a serious tone. "It's going to be OK, Herb. It truly is. Don't step away from this awesome gift." He turned his head slightly for effect.

Herb pursed his lips in thought. "Exactly what do you have to do with what I'm going through anyway?"

"I don't know, Herb. I just do what's put on my heart. Trust me, I am not trying to change you or influence you. It's not me, Herb. But it *is* someone." Herb sighed. He seemed to do that a lot these last few weeks. If anything, it was truly selfless and kind of Harry to go along, not questioning why.

"Herb, just go with it. There's a train taking you somewhere. Stay on it until the last station. OK?" Herb liked the metaphor. He nodded and smiled at Harry, slapping the roof of the car and turned to go home for his Sunday dinner. "See you bright and early!" Harry yelled out as he deftly managed a U-turn and resumed his drive along Lake Avenue. A breeze suddenly swept through, blowing dust from the street up and away. Herb thought he saw a small manila card in the debris flying by.

June was peeling some potatoes to add to the oven for the last forty-five minutes or so while the roast finished. A bed of carrots and celery supporting the beef were already more than well done but helped to make a wonderful au jus to accompany the meal. Herb took off his jacket and hung his hat on the wall rack next to his Magic Dairy hat. He contemplated his work hat for a moment, then picked up the Sunday paper to try and relax while June finished fussing with the meal. He pondered the ups and downs of his emotions over the last few weeks. In a moment of awareness, he understood that it must be difficult for June. Her pure kindness towards him made Herb feel remorseful.

Not saying anything, June walked in and handed Herb a small glass of tomato juice and simply smiled. Herb patted her hand. She was such a treasure; so good to him, so gentle in her ways. He certainly didn't deserve her. He thought he didn't deserve this "gift" he was experiencing, either. Why him? Why now? What did it mean? What was he supposed to do next? The questions kept coming. The answers did not.

The meal was consumed in silence other than Herb murmuring something about how much he was enjoying the tender beef and especially the au jus on his potatoes. June told him to take his time and enjoy it.

The meal finished; Herb turned on the radio to catch the last of the Yankees game on WINS. He enjoyed listening to Phil Rizzuto, the "Scooter" as he joined the broadcast team that year, replacing Jim Woods. Phil brought clarity and innocent enthusiasm to the game, intermingling personal anecdotes with the action on the diamond. Mel Allen and Red Barber were the consummate broadcast pros, and Phil was the kid who called the game in wonder of what he was seeing and reporting. The trio rotated and took turns on the TV and the radio, but Herb preferred hearing the game on the radio. No one could paint a mental picture of the game like Mel and Red and with Phil's overripe, wide-eyed enthusiasm, it made for wonderful listening. Hearing the legendary Bob Sheppard announce the players in the background was the ultimate cherry on top.

As a young boy, my own interests as you know by now were primarily centered on anything having to do with fishing and baseball. On a Sunday afternoon drive through Western Connecticut, the Yankees would be on the car radio as my dad wandered up Route 7 to Kent Falls or over to Lake Lillinoah while my sister and I admired the scenery. If I had heroes, they were Yankees players; Yogi Berra, Mickey Mantle, Moose Skowron, Elston Howard ... I could name the starting lineups, the bullpen, the pinch hitters and possibly the bat boys.

With our nickels and dimes found, saved or earned, we kids from the neighborhood would buy packs of Topps baseball cards at the Rogers Park Pharmacy and snap the flat piece of gum in half, chewing it while we perused our new treasures, eagerly downing statistics and player biographies. Emulating the major-league players, I wrapped my mitt around a well-used baseball and secured it with a huge rubber band until the fielder's glove held a perfect shape. I bent down the corners of my cap just like the big leaguers. The fact that I was far removed from being any sort of athlete did not dissuade me from my fantasy. As one of the bigger kids in the neighborhood, when we played sandlot ball against some kids from the other side of Rogers Park, they'd see me step up to the plate and the outfielders would back up, expecting me to smash the ball. Occasionally I would, but more often, I'd hit a soft line drive or grounder. I was not very well-coordinated, kind of all knees and elbows, and was usually dispatched to play right field, supposedly the most harmless place to put such a mediocre ballplayer.

My Christmas prayers were answered that year with the great gift of a transistor radio so I could listen to my team whenever I wanted, and in the years to come to follow Bruce Morrow on WABC as he spun top 40 hits to help me through long winter evenings, the radio speaker laying atop my ear. When April came around, I imagined myself in the mezzanine announcer's booth at Yankee Stadium, as I imitated Bob Sheppard's voice, introducing the players as they came to bat. His voice, his style was perfectly unique and never ever reproduced by any announcer anywhere. To even attempt to do so would have been blasphemous. "Now batting ... the centerfielder ... number seven ... Mickey ... Mantle." The pace, the inflection. To me, Bob Sheppard *was* baseball.

Herb rose from his chair as the game concluded with a Yankees win, fueled by Mickey Mantle and his MVP-winning season. Herb was mildly satisfied and happy. He had been distracted for about an hour; it was enough to clear his mind. Later, gently kissing his bride of ten years goodnight, Herb fell into a gentle sleep hearing the lovely music in his head fading to a coda: "Now batting ... the catcher ... number eight ... Yogi ... Berra."

As usual, it was dark as the inside of a coffin at 4 a.m. Monday morning but Herb felt like a million bucks, having slept soundly and completely. He did his best to tiptoe through the house guided by a couple of night lights as he prepared for work, putting on the coffee and making himself a hard roll with butter. A hard roll and butter plus a cup of coffee fueled a large part of the Danbury area's workforce and Herb was no exception. He moved easily and quietly around the kitchen thinking about what Harry had said; "Just go with it." Today's route meant driving the new Divco and the possibility of a "trip." Herb decided he would give it another chance and as Harry urged, to get on that train; to go with it.

Chapter Twenty-Six

"The fruit of the Spirit is kindness..."

Herb was in a cheerful mood despite the early hour. Some people claimed that one could never get used to rising so early every morning; that the circadian rhythms needed those last few hours of darkness and sleep to nurture good health. Herb didn't buy into all that. He was used to it after so many years delivering dairy and since he usually got half the afternoon off, he felt better about his position than if he worked a regular day shift and had to fight whatever traffic Danbury offered at 5:30 in the afternoon.

The only thing Herb lamented about his job was working six days. Attending a Saturday afternoon game at Yankee Stadium was out of the question. Even if the Yankees had a night game scheduled, after being up at 4 a.m., there was no way Herb would last until late in the evening and then have to drive an hour or more home. But he had the radio and the wonderful, genteel and knowledgeable broadcasters who brought each game alive. That would have to do.

The emotional roller-coaster ride Herb had been on was back on the upswing. Harry had made sense. He kept it simple. "Stay on the train; see where it takes you." Herb decided he could do that.

Things were changing in 1957. Though they didn't watch much television, Herb and June both enjoyed *The Lucy Show* but sadly, the last episode aired in early May. Elvis Presley was still gaining in popularity and a squadron of B-52 bombers made an around the world trip in just over 40 hours. There was a lot to consider and frankly, to worry about with the Soviets rattling swords, but through it all, Herb continued to enjoy his soothing baseball games on the radio and reading all the scores and stories in the News-Times. All sixteen major league teams were of interest, even the lowly Senators and Pirates who as it would turn out in a scheduling coincidence that year, ended up playing in the final games at both Ebbets Field and the Polo Grounds as the Dodgers and Giants abandoned New York for warmer climes and presumably more money-making opportunities in California.

The route today was uninspiring. Herb made a few extra sales, he lost a few. What made time pass quickly was thinking about his upcoming lunch break. With no clue what was about to happen or to what time period or where he would go, Herb rolled up to the elm tree next to the pond and shut down the Divco. He hesitated; not sure if he was really in the mood. Sighing, he obeyed Harry's admonition to "go with it," and so he did. He got out of the truck to the sound of joyful children jumping around at the new trampoline park. It was good to be young. Thinking ahead, Herb hoped it would be good to be old as well. He took the manila card, blank of course, and stepped back into the truck where everything became white.

Herb found himself in an office at Magic Dairy that was not nearly as impressive as that of Mr. Mark but was quite surprised seeing his name on a desk nameplate with the underscoring phrase, "Operations Director." A promotion! He looked around from the comfort of an executive chair. Operations Director ... must have been a result of his hard work and accuracy with finances and that was true, but it didn't hurt one bit that when the job came open, it was the fact that Frank Mark simply liked Herb that helped sway the hiring decision. Herb's office was decorated with a small Christmas tree and cheerily lighted garland strung around the windowsill. A framed photograph of June that was unfamiliar to Herb graced the corner of the metal desk.

Despite the enjoyment he derived from driving a route and at least partially being his own boss, Herb thought that the perks of the office job must be pretty good, such as not having to arise at 4 a.m. each day and the ability to work a five-day week. If this is what the future held workwise, he was ready for it. Two newspapers on his desk, the News-Times and The New York Times gave away the date: Friday, December 22, 1972. Mr. Mark's assistant Betty stuck her head in the door.

"Remember, half-day today Mr. Lundy and the party starts at eleven." Herb smiled and nodded his understanding.

A nice long Christmas weekend awaited and Herb in his momentary reverie looked forward to it, while simultaneously remembering he was just a visitor to this time with no control over what would happen and how long this visit would last.

His desk revealed little work that needed to be done, and nothing of any urgency on the eve of the holiday awaited so he opened up the News-Times to the sports section. Among the basketball and football scores and predictions, he came across a yearly summary of baseball and a look ahead towards spring training including a mention of Danbury's own Joe Lahoud, playing for the Milwaukee Brewers. Brewers? What about the Braves? Curious, but still, a Danbury native in the big leagues was kind of neat.

Further reading revealed the league now consisted of twenty-four teams and something called a league championship series instead of simply two pennant winners. Herb's beloved Yankees had fallen to mediocrity barely managing a winning season while in the National

League, the Pirates had elevated to division winners but had lost in a playoff round to Cincinnati.

A recap of Danbury High School's football season included a team photo in front of an unfamiliar building and an ad for last-minute shoppers at someplace called the Danbury Mall was another eye-opener. Well, of course, things change, businesses come and go, people move on or pass away. So, no surprises that a newspaper fifteen years in the future would reveal changes such as these.

Feeling a wave of sleepiness, Herb elected to sit back and close his eyes for just a moment. When he came around, Herb was standing outside Ed's Cigar Box on Main Street holding Saturday's late edition of the New York Times. He'd moved on to the next day. A front-page headline proclaimed, "Thousands Dead as Quakes Strike Nicaraguan City."

The article described crumpled buildings, water mains broken, and fires throughout the devastated capital of Managua. A report indicated possibly 18,000 dead, many more injured and 200,000 left homeless. An incredible disaster. Neighboring countries immediately responded with relief supplies although getting into the area was nearly impossible as refugees flooded the roads trying to escape the ruins and the fires.

Herb was deeply troubled and moved by the tremendous disaster. The Red Cross of course leaped into action and donations were being solicited by numerous organizations across the globe to bring desperately needed relief supplies to the stricken country.

Among those leading the collection efforts was Roberto Clemente of the Pirates, now a certified major league star. Herb remembered seeing his name as an up-and-coming player. Clemente took on the role leading a major relief organization due to his familiarity with and love for Nicaragua, a country that hosted his visiting Puerto Rican all-star team in the recent Amateur Baseball World Series tournament. The country reminded Roberto of growing up in Puerto Rico; simpler times and the people warmly welcomed Roberto and his team.

Herb drifted in and out of awareness of his days in late 1972. One moment, he was reading a newspaper account of an earthquake disaster, the next in a state of semi-consciousness, unsure of what was happening or why he was still in 1972. It was as if the cards of these days were being shuffled with Herb a passenger to the task.

He dimly recalled seeing sleek cars, some of which had engines that reminded him of the noisy flathead Ford racing engines at the Racearena. Loud exhausts, big tires and car names like Oldsmobile 4-4-2, a Chevrolet

Chevelle SS, something called a Camaro 496, and a boldly decorated Pontiac G-T-O that looked fast standing still. He faintly recalled hearing radio stations playing songs that told stories like "Me and Mrs. Jones," and "I am Woman," by someone named Helen Reddy. A movie titled, "The Godfather" seemed to be quite popular and newspaper articles mentioned an upcoming football game called the "Superbowl."

Herb had no recollection of staying overnight anywhere or experiencing anything noteworthy over the course of a few calendar days. He was in a transitioning dreamlike state and in more lucid moments, wondered if he'd somehow become stuck in 1972.

His next moment of awareness was in his office at Magic Dairy, the morning of January 2, 1973, the first workday of the new year. On his desk, the New York Times reported some very sad news: "Clemente, Pirates' Star, Dies in Crash Of Plane Carrying Aid to Nicaragua."

Stunned, Herb read the piece. It was sickening. After having led fundraising efforts including personally going door-to-door to collect donations for Nicaraguan relief and after having found that three previous planeloads of relief supplies he'd coordinated had been intercepted by the Nicaraguan military for profiteering, Clemente was so moved and so disgusted by the thievery that he vowed to personally help load and deliver a fourth plane-load of supplies and medicine directly from Puerto Rico to Managua.

In an ultimate act of kindness towards fellow human beings, Roberto Clemente climbed aboard an overloaded and aging DC-7 cargo plane determined that this particular load of supplies would reach those most in need. Vera Clemente worried that the plane looked old and overloaded. Roberto assured his dear wife all was well and not to worry. Tragically, an engine exploded shortly after takeoff and while attempting to circle back for an emergency landing, the doomed plane crashed a mile and a half offshore in heavy seas. There were no survivors.

Herb looked up from the article, shaken, not only by the tragedy but by the incredible selflessness shown by someone who hadn't needed to become so deeply involved but must have had it placed on his heart to help. Mr. Clemente could have simply written a check and urged others do to so but was so moved by the humanitarian crisis that personal involvement was his only course. Thinking back, Herb vaguely recalled part of a sermon in which Reverend Waller had mentioned the notion of biblical kindness, that "Christians should show kindness by behaving toward others as God has behaved toward them." Indeed.

Much more than being known as a baseball star, Roberto Clemente had made the supreme sacrifice for his fellow human beings, in what was an ultimate act of kindness.

Sighing deeply, sobbing nearly, Herb looked around his future office, wondering if this office and this job were shadows of things that would happen or might happen. That seemed to matter little in this profound moment of awareness. Breathing deeply, Herb reached for and touched the little manila card deep in his pocket and was instantly returned to 1957 and the magically configured Divco delivery truck.

Chapter Twenty-Seven

The fruit of the Spirit is goodness..."

A large portion of the population hated
Mondays because they represented a new work
week after having had the opportunity to enjoy
60 hours to themselves. Herb didn't mind at all,
particularly since it was a day when he would
command the new Divco truck, the one with the
small gold plate under the hood and the magical
power to transport him to another time. Having
struggled with self-doubt, Herb was more serene
now thanks to Harry's supportive comments and
the quiet understanding from his wife. Herb was
now fully on board, looking forward to today's
lunchtime break, and his trip ... somewhere.

Something was different this morning in
May. The air was a bit warmer and the trees had
aggressively sprouted their new mantle of leaves.
The road crews were finishing up their pothole
repair duties, most of the smudge pots having
been gathered up and stored for another season.
Children across town were eagerly anticipating
summer vacation from school while parents
finalized arrangements to spend a week or two
along the coast somewhere or perhaps at a lodge
in the Berkshires. Herb thought of his own two-
week holiday, but it would not come until

September when the kids were back in school and vacation spots less crowded. Driving along his route, his mind wandered to consider the possibilities; perhaps a trip to the Maine coast or an extended visit to Gettysburg and a few other Civil War battlefields. He was on automatic pilot, making deliveries, selling some extra dairy products and cheerfully, almost leisurely spending a few extra minutes chatting with his customers. The ones who noticed saw a peacefulness with Herb in place of his usual super-energy and apparent fitfulness.

Enjoying a slower pace on his morning run, Herb elected to put aside his penchant for timing himself and instead decided that enjoying every moment was much more valuable than racing from one stop to the next. It felt different. It felt good. He even took the time to listen to the ramblings of one of the cafeteria workers at South Street School, the one that was generally ignored if not made fun of by her co-workers. Herb just smiled, listened patiently to the roundabout story and then patted the woman on her shoulder in a random moment of compassion that brought a broad smile to the woman who otherwise and routinely wore a scornful look.

Putting off the rest of the southern route until after lunch, Herb put the Divco into gear and eased his way back on to South Street, making an immediate left at the broad intersection with Main Street into Rogers Park. Crossing the first stone bridge over a small creek, Herb pulled over for a moment and got out to admire the pure craftsmanship of the structure he'd driven over and ignored a thousand times. It was carefully assembled by a father and son team as a WPA project in the 1930s and judging from the structure, would last well beyond Herb's lifetime. Every stone was carefully selected and placed; the cement grout neatly trimmed and pointed. The gentle arch held a prominent keystone and the stonework was topped by a smooth and thick cement ledge. It was as much a work of art as it was a functional bridge. Herb wondered how many other ordinary things he passed by every day, never stopping to appreciate their historical context and true value.

Herb breathed deeply. The air was sweet with the scent of blooming flowers. It was too early for the rose trellises to come into their glory, but the dogwood trees and cherry blossoms were out as were spring daffodils and crabapples. Birds brightly and cheerfully chirped, winging from one tree to another while unseen bees did their work. Herb pondered the wonder of it all and the diversity of life that surrounded him in complexity that was if nothing else, astounding. He put the Divco into gear and continued down to the elm tree at the pond.

Herb brought the Divco to a halt in his

usual spot and looking up did not see a manila card stuck in the crook of the tree branch. Instead, there was a book. A book! Looking around, Herb stepped out of the truck and walked over to the familiar elm. He could make out the title of the book – "Mere Christianity" by C.S. Lewis. This could be no mistake or coincidence. C.S. Lewis was the atheist become theist, a believer and one whose observations were not of a religious fanatic with an agenda but one who came to faith on a rough and tumble road. Herb knew of him but had not read him. But he understood the significance of finding this book in place of the usual manila card. He grabbed the book and returned to the truck. All became white.

Herb found himself in a parlor of sorts, perhaps a meeting room at some hotel or a community center. There were eight-panel windows at shoulder level for those seated in the gallery and Herb noticed a double-decker red bus pass by, traveling in the opposite lane. A man seated next to him had a copy of *The Daily Telegraph* dated May 14, 1947. It became clear to Herb; he was in London. He gathered himself and looked around the room. It held ten rows of folding chairs and about 80 or so people attending a talk or presentation of some sort. At the podium stood a man who worked for the BBC in the religious broadcasting division. He was speaking about an author who was the subject of the meeting.

"Now, the case for morality is one of the most fascinating subjects at hand, with the perspective of the author transmogrifying from atheist to theist, within his own consciousness. That itself is rather startling but the clarity in which he is able to convey, with absolute certainty the validity of morality not as a contrivance of man but as an immutable power of nature is simply stunning." The book in Herb's hand felt warm to the touch. The speaker continued.

"Now, you might say yes, but still, how can morality be a law when it is so commonly broken? And here is the genius of the proposition. If you take nothing else away from today's talk, take this. Lewis argued that morality is known intuitively. He gives the example that thirst reflects the fact that people naturally need water, and there is no other substance that satisfies that need. We can all agree on that, can we not?" The speaker surveyed the room and finding no resistance to his proposition continued. "It is a force of nature so to speak. Are you with me?" Heads nodded. "Lewis explained for example that earthly experience does not satisfy the human craving for 'joy' and that only God could provide true joy. Despite the Hitlers of the world, people seek unseen things like joy and love and goodness. Lewis makes the point:

Humans cannot know to yearn for something if it does not exist. Therefore, morality must exist. It does exist. You cannot see it, nor touch it, nor smell it but it is there. It is intuitive, it is naturally occurring and so it exists, just as thirst exists."

Herb sat back in his chair. He murmured the quote in his head: "Humans cannot know to yearn for something if it does not exist." The sentence rolled around in his head. Do we yearn for love? Yes. Do we yearn for kindness? Do we yearn for joy? For gentleness? Yes, yes, and yes. We yearn for things unseen, yet they exist. We yearn in the same way for our Creator. Our Father. The great I Am. Herb breathed deeply. He thought of a sermon in which the Reverend Waller had said, "Only God is Good." Indeed. We may yearn for goodness and not quite achieve it, but we know of one who is truly Good. With morality a law of nature then according to C.S. Lewis, we are certainly drawn to goodness, however short of it we may fall.

Bringing the talk to a close, the speaker stepped from the podium to a warm round of applause as several attendees lined up to say a word. The man with the newspaper touched Herb's sleeve and pointed towards the book.

"I've read it twice. I still don't grasp everything, but it's truly changed my life. Bryan Thompson." The man extended his hand. Herb shook it. "Herb Lundy."

"I've actually just started reading it." The man looked at Herb's odd attire; odd for the Kensington borough anyway.

"Well, I'm off. Enjoy the book!"

"Thank you. I will. Nice meeting you." Herb's gaze followed the man out the door to the busy street. He walked outside. Evidence of the blitz was still apparent. After all, how could the area suffer more than 33,000 homes destroyed and be restored within just a few years? The answer was obvious.

London was coming back, slowly. The war was two years distant, but people were still compelled to do things like eating horse meat. The Thames flooded as a result of excess snowfall from an unusually harsh winter. Disabled veterans worked in makeshift factories making poppies, while football got back in gear with great vigor as eager fans stood by their teams, crowding into the legendary stadiums to see their heroes battle on the pitch.

Herb remembered how he had helped defend this island, these people. Despite the horrors of battle and the hardships, he felt a solemn pride in having been part of it, and by extension, part of this slow restoration. The people of Britain yearned for peace and now it was real. They yearned for normalcy. Normalcy was upon them and growing. Herb sat on a park bench and opened his book. A manila card marked a page. Halfway down the page, the line read, "Humans cannot know to yearn for something if it does not exist." Herb's mind wandered to the last words of a Psalm, "Surely, goodness and mercy shall follow me all the days of my life." Herb touched the manila card and returned home.

Humans cannot know to yearn for something if it does not exist.

Chapter Twenty-Eight

The fruit of the Spirit is faithfulness..."

Summer meant fewer sales, lower commissions, and more challenges in being able to pay the bills. A good number of Herb's customers would leave town for two weeks, even longer, as they played in the Catskills, wandered the coastline of Maine or suffered each other's company on long car rides to the Midwest. A customer who was on the road was not a customer who needed milk, cream or cottage cheese and so Herb's income dropped accordingly. Fortunately, there were no heating bills to pay, winter clothes to buy nor snow tires to mount. The shortage of customers meant shorter days on the road as well.

The time trips continued although Herb didn't pick up the manila card every time it was presented. It seemed to make sense to absorb what lesson had been experienced before moving on to the next one if he could. Had this been a problem, Herb was sure he'd be given a sign or some message and there was none. Time apparently, was on his side.

On this summer Monday however, Herb was ready to venture forth once more. His ability to choose a time or place was shaky at best and it wasn't clear exactly how what thought or vision he had, and when he had it would trigger the time trip. There was no outfoxing the process but still, he wondered if he could pick and choose.

Sweating through his work shirt, Herb's mind drifted to a winter's day with Christmas around the corner, the lights adorning Danbury's Main Street aglow with the distinctive stars draped across the wide avenue. Genung's and Feinson's would be busy with shoppers, and good cheer would be evident even in the surliest of shopkeepers or railway agents. Herb thought he would trade today's tropical heat for a bracing cold breeze, even a snow or sleet storm.

Putting the yearning for winter aside, Herb focused on the job. His angle today was to sell eggs and lots of them. Summer meant picnics and days at Sherwood Island State Park and what goes better at a picnic or day at the beach than homemade potato salad topped with hard-boiled egg slices adorned with paprika? That was his pitch to anyone who was home at the time of his delivery, and it was fairly successful. Of course, he bypassed Edna's customers thereby avoiding her wrath but managed to sell an extra eight dozen eggs to housewives who embraced Herb's picnic vision, and charming smile. If they didn't warm up to the idea of buying extra eggs, Herb hit them with the other summer treat – homemade ice cream. Of course, that would require heavy cream, some of which he had in his truck. How many pints would they need?

Herb didn't time his routes in the summer. There was no sport to it since he'd beat every standing record within one week. Having sold out his truck for the day, Herb guided the Divco with the small gold plate down Memorial Drive all the way to Rogers Park Pond and the big elm tree under which he'd enjoy his lunch. He ate his sandwich while staring at a manila card tucked into the "V" shaped notch where a branch spanned out from the trunk. Should he take it today? Yes, it felt right.

After the bright white faded, Herb was able to focus on his surroundings. He found himself in a classroom or maybe it was a library space. There were small chairs lined up and some kind of electronic device with blinking lights on it mounted near the wall. It wasn't a slide projector or a movie projector that he knew of and it did have a lens of sorts on the front, but it was way too small to be a movie projector.

"OK kids settle down. Settle down." Herb then noticed the background din of twenty children all talking at once as they slowly quieted down for the teacher, if that's what she was. "Let's all welcome Santa," as she pointed towards Herb who further noticed he was sweating and wearing a red suit. Oh, golly.

The lady who was a teacher or maybe a

community center volunteer nodded towards "Santa" as if to indicate it was his turn to speak. She pointed to a piece of paper next to the generously sized chair in which he was sitting as the children cheered his presence. He read from the page. "Hi kids!" Instinctively he knew that enthusiasm was required despite his confusion. The children replied with a robust, "Hi Santa!"

"Welcome to the special showing today of 'The Santa Clause' and don't forget, we're doing presents after the movie!" Cheers arose. The teacher or volunteer dimmed the room lights as the children excitedly awaited the movie.

"You can take a break now if you want," the teacher spoke into Herb's ear.

"No, that's OK. I think I'll watch the movie with the kids. Uh, when did this movie come out?"

"Oh, you know. Last year, 1994." OK, now Herb knew when he was, but wasn't sure where he was. Without knowing why, Herb felt that he was probably near a downtown urban area. The joy on the kids' faces was priceless, well worth the trip all by itself. Such unspoiled love, such raw faith.

The movie began, the story of a reluctant businessman who is magically transformed into the next Santa Claus due to having scared the current Santa off his roof causing an injury from which the man would not recover. A business card recovered from Santa's coat pocket contained in the fine print the agreement now forged between the finder of the card and his obligation to become the new Santa Claus – in other words, the Santa "Clause."

Herb enjoyed the movie but was noticeably impressed by two particular scenes. In the first one, as the new Santa is shepherded away to the North Pole, he is shown to his room to get some rest along with his son, Charlie who accompanied him on the previous night's rounds. An elf brings in some hot cocoa for him to drink and as he looks out the window he remarks, "Is that a polar bear directing traffic down there? I see it, but I don't believe it."

Judy the elf replies, "You're missing the point."

"What is the point?"

"Seeing isn't believing; believing is seeing."

Herb pondered the scene. Straight out of the book of John chapter 20 verse 25: *"The other disciples, therefore, said unto him, we have seen the Lord. But he said unto them, Except I shall see in his hands the print of the nails and put my finger into the print of the nails, and thrust my hand into his side, I will not believe."* The dilemma and the words of Thomas. Doubting Thomas. Then, John 20 verse 27-29: *"Then saith he to Thomas, reach hither thy finger, and behold my hands; and reach hither thy hand, and thrust it into my side: and be not faithless, but believing. [28] And Thomas answered and said unto him, My Lord and my God. [29] Jesus saith unto him, Thomas, because thou hast seen me, thou hast believed: blessed are they that have not seen, and yet have believed."*

The scene overwhelmed Herb. He missed the next few moments of the movie. Of course. Believing is seeing. That's the key. Later in the movie, Charlie attempts to explain his Christmas Eve adventure to his stepfather, a psychiatrist attempting to bring Charlie back to reality. A reality, it could be argued, lacking in faith and relying only upon face value. After grilling Charlie about how it's possible for Santa to visit a home with no chimney, and how could one man possibly deliver presents to children around the world in one night, he confidently delivers what he thinks is the settling argument: "Have you ever seen a reindeer fly?"

Charlie responds, "Yes. Have you ever seen a million dollars?" The stepfather replies that he has not. Belying his young age, Charlie confidently declares, "Just because you haven't seen it doesn't mean it doesn't exist."

Such wisdom in a children's movie. Herb was reassured, satisfied. The movie, of course, had a happy and predictable ending but it was the two scenes that stuck with Herb. He told the group of precious five- and six-year-old children that it was OK to believe, that delightful things only happen when you free yourself to wonder, to be faithful. He didn't step on anyone's now politically correct toes, nor did he shy from giving these kids permission to nurture faith. Without faith, after all, there are no prayers answered, no salvation by grace, and no pleasing God. There is no climbing into an airplane without faith that it's well-built and the pilot is skilled and experienced. There is no eating food from the market without faith that it's been properly handled and good to eat. Herb reflected upon the fact that we don't think about faith in day-to-day situations, but it's there all the same. So why should it be limited to airplanes and food? Herb knew he was right.

Presents were handed out to children with wonder in their eyes and if they were not conscious of it, thankful hearts. Someone cared enough to bring them joy. Someone had faith that they deserved this moment. The wrapping paper collected, and toys opened, Herb stepped towards the door, glancing out the window for the first time. A large harbor town. Portland Maine, perhaps. He liked Maine. Herb sighed heavily, touched the manila card, and everything once again became white.

Chapter Twenty-Nine

"The fruit of the Spirit is gentleness..."

It was a warm Monday morning as Herb slipped the special Divco truck out of the Magic Dairy parking lot. Still dark, the ambitious headlights of the Divco marked the way as Herb eased past the volunteer fire department and the immediate sharp corner that was close alongside a wedge-shaped outparcel of the Danbury municipal airport. The Divco had service last week and was running strong. Herb passed a low building on the left he knew to be the shop and office of Robert L. Dingee, a brilliant and crusty engineer who spent World War II dissecting army tanks and telling the government how to fix them. A brilliant mind, he proved more valuable in perfecting weapons designs than toting an M1 across the hedgerows of France.

The plucky Divco crossed Route 7, the main artery leading south to Wilton and Norwalk or north past New Milford all the way beyond Kent Falls up to the Massachusetts border. Miry Brook Road turned into the twisting and hilly Wooster Heights. Wooster Heights, in turn, became simply Wooster Street as the road coursed through residential neighborhoods eventually crossing Deer Hill Avenue and finishing downhill towards Main Street.

Herb had a special request from his boss, Frank Mark, to drop off extra milk and heavy cream so he turned the Divco left onto Deer Hill Avenue and crept to a stop at the Mark residence. Silently leaving the order in the shiny galvanized box, he returned to the milk truck to start his regular run. He passed the imposing structure of the First Congregational Church on the left before turning on to West Street and then heading south on Main. The church was a magnificent sight, even in the early morning shadows before dawn's first light. For reasons unknown, Herb thought to leave an extra five-dollar bill in the silver-trimmed offering plate next Sunday.

The route continued as usual, with Herb marking the time and staying on schedule as the eager Divco routed him from one home to the next. As the morning wore on, he began to see customers who were now awake or heading out to work. Mrs. Johnson on Putnam Drive eagerly greeted Herb as he made his twice-weekly delivery and took a moment to thank him for no particular reason other than always providing friendly, reliable service and taking time to chat with an old lady who appreciated some company from time to time. She gave him an envelope with a bill inside.

"You buy yourself a nice lunch with this, Herb. Thank you for doing such a great job."

Herb was slightly embarrassed by the attention and thanked the sweet lady for the tip saying it wasn't necessary, but she insisted. Herb tucked the envelope with Mr. Lincoln on the bill into his pocket and proceeded onward.

With two dozen homes left to serve, Herb decided to take a break at 11:45 a.m. and take his lunch at the park. There hadn't been a manila card in the last couple of weeks and Herb wondered if he'd done something wrong or maybe the lesson was over. He didn't feel like it was over because he'd not knowingly had any sort of complete revelation. All the same, he dutifully parked under the tree and saw the card awaiting him. Anxious to see where the adventure might lead today, he skipped lunch and grabbed the card from the tree. As usual, a slight breeze kicked up and the pond came alive with little wavelets. Stepping back into the truck, everything became white.

It was chilly. That's the first thing Herb noticed, and he was surrounded by a crowd of people standing in a semi-circle around a makeshift stage. Most of the men wore top hats of some sort and others were dressed in what looked like authentic Civil War uniforms complete with gold braids and swords at their sides. The women wore ground-length dresses and homemade sweaters. Herb could see trees shorn of leaves and some torn apart by what looked to have been a violent storm. A steeple could be seen not far away along with another building with an interesting looking cupola. It seemed to be about noontime near as Herb could tell as the crowd buzzed at the arrival of a slender tall man, one of the few not wearing a hat. Herb guessed he was at some sort of dedication and an important one at that if the man he saw was who he suspected he might be.

Printed programs were being passed around the crowd and Herb was handed one. It was a very old-fashioned printing style and ornate. The top line read, "Order of Procession," followed by, "For the Inauguration of the National Cemetery at Gettysburg, Pa. on the 19th, November 1863." All Herb could think of was Phil Rizzuto's response to anything unusual or wonderful: "Holy cow."

The page offered a complete and lengthy list of dignitaries and participants. Page two provided the Order of Exercises including a highly detailed list of various military movements and placements during the morning that would precede the speeches and prayers. It detailed every aspect of how and where the military units would proceed to their positions and where the civic procession would advance, eventually occupying the front area of the stand. Herb noticed with interest that ladies would occupy the right of the stand while politely and firmly suggesting they be in place by no later than 10 a.m. Finally, the exercises were described in order:

> Music
> Prayer
> Music
> Oration
> Music
> Remarks by President of the United States
> Dirge
> Benediction

It was well regarded at the time that the oration to be given by the stateman Edward Everett would be the highlight of the day; a long and detailed story of the battle to be skillfully presented by the esteemed Everett who carefully constructed his speech including details drawn from his personal interviews with those involved in the great struggle. Lincoln's address was to be the brief dedication of the cemetery. As history would have it, the "real" Gettysburg Address was overshadowed by the brief remarks of the President, a 10-sentence speech since memorized by every student in Herb's time.

Herb was amazed. To be witness to the actual events of this day was beyond any expectation. Ninety minutes into the presentation by Edward Everett, Herb knew why Lincoln's address was the one remembered and revered through the years. Finishing his lengthy oration took Everett no less than two hours as the crowd shifted their weight and wondered just how long a man could talk. Make no mistake, Everett was a brilliant orator, and his points made were well researched and informative. Truth be told, a lengthy oration was not unusual for the day.

More music followed by the U.S. Marine Band, then Mr. Lincoln took the stage. In a few short minutes, he captured the heart and the soul of what had transpired on that bloody ground just four months prior. His style was steady and measured. Each word was weighted and carried its own meaning. The crowd was silent; stunned even upon hearing the brilliant commentary from one who was truly a gentle man. In humility, he beseeched the listeners to mark his words and honor those who had given every measure of devotion to a just cause. He finished his short speech:

"It is rather for us to be here dedicated to the great task remaining before us — that from these honored dead we take increased devotion to that cause for which they gave the last full measure of devotion — that we here highly resolve that these dead shall not have died in vain — that this nation, under God, shall have a new birth of freedom — and that government of the people, by the people, for the people, shall not perish from the earth."

The speech literally gave Herb goosebumps. Rather than a robust ovation from the assembled crowd, there was a stunned silence, a smattering of applause and a few cheers. Such weighty words had probably not been heard in the lifetimes of any of these men, women, soldiers, and politicians. The speech was delivered in such a measured pace that a reporter for the Associated Press was able to transcribe every word. It was as if the nation stopped momentarily, to reset itself, to resolve to move ahead while honoring those lost in the desperate struggle that took so many lives while setting the course for the remainder of the war.

Lincoln thought the brief speech a failure owing to the lack of reaction by the crowd. He had been feeling ill leading up to the event and considered that to be a factor. The next day, however, a letter from Edward Everett praised Lincoln's dedication speech claiming that the President had accomplished in two short minutes what he himself had failed to achieve in some two hours. It was lofty praise from one who had the expertise to recognize what had just occurred.

Unlike the others, Herb knew how history would treat those 272 words and how they became the marrow of the soul of a nation for decades to come. As the crowd dispersed, Herb was able to contemplate what he had just witnessed. Having the advantage of knowing the history that followed, he came to appreciate the genius of Lincoln more than ever before.

Above all traits, it was Lincoln's humility, such as in naming his Republican presidential rivals to his cabinet, and his ability to convey such a humble yet eternally powerful message, that defined the man.

Herb knew from sitting in the first pew at First Congregational Church that the fruit of the Spirit known as gentleness was meant to convey the notion of strength through humility, just as Jesus rode into Jerusalem on the back of a donkey instead of a team of horses riding a gold chariot. Even in his ultimate greatness, Jesus humbly entered the town that would crucify him days later. To try and assign oneself to that depth of a gentle spirit was beyond human comprehension.

Herb remembered the envelope in his pocket. Was it still there? Yes, his five-dollar bill was securely tucked away. Would the speaker have been amused if Herb had taken it out and revealed it to the crowd? Fortunately, that was not the type of stunt Herb would perform. Tired from standing and now noticeably thirsty, Herb touched the manila card and found himself back in the Divco. It took several moments before he could gather himself to continue his route.

Ricky and I had been fishing at the pond at Rogers Park without much luck. Midday was not the ideal time to fish but we had the nightcrawlers and the day to ourselves so why not give it a try? I noticed the milk truck under the tree. I recognized Mr. Lundy from church and the Main Street Bake Shop. He looked a bit dazed. There was that breeze a moment ago, and then it stopped as quickly as it started. Then, I heard the truck motor start and as it did, both of our bobbers disappeared with a jolt under the surface of the pond. Fish on!

Chapter Thirty

"The fruit of the Spirit is self-control..."

Herb was not oblivious to the sequence of time trips he was taking and the meaning behind each one. The first trip, which seemed long ago, back to his B-24 bomber is when he was reminded of love; not casual love but what they call "agape" love. The highest form of love, agape love was thought to be the love by God for man and by man for God. A love that transcends, regardless of any circumstance. He remembered Reverend Waller talking about it once, but it seemed too arcane a concept at the time. So, when he transported back to his gunner's position and opted not to fire upon and most likely kill that Luftwaffe pilot, despite the circumstances and directives of war, it was his moment of agape love. This he considered on the warmish Thursday morning while downing a second cup of Maxwell House coffee. The special Divco truck was his today. Would there be one more adventure in it?

During the course of his travels, Herb surveyed the trips he'd taken. The agape love was clear, then there was the utter and simple joy of that World War I airman's family. The next experience was a lesson in peace. Yes, he was on

187

a trip living out the fruit of the Spirit, just as they were described and sequenced in Galatians Chapter 5, Verse 22. Feeling clever that he had recognized what was happening, Herb was still short on how it would all tie together. This Thursday, if a card was placed in the elm tree, the sequence would dictate that the trip would be about self-control. It was the last of the nine. He wondered what if any part of his memory or experience, or future fantasy would come into play this time. Sighing, he realized he wouldn't know until the moment arrived. Herb climbed into the Ford to make his way once again to Magic Dairy.

Good old "Bucko" had loaded half his truck by the time Herb arrived. Not necessary. Harry was sweating even in the darkness of the early morning hour. It was the humidity. Not one to complain, he simply carried a hand towel with him to wipe his brow now and then. He greeted Herb with what one could describe as something of a knowing smirk; an unspoken secret known to Harry but not yet to Herb.

Herb grabbed a few cheesecloth bags of ice and began icing down the milk bottles and other products and Harry continued to heft them into their slots. "Looks like a pretty hot one today, huh Harry?"

"Already is, Herb. Look at me." Herb was right. Harry's shirt was nearly soaked in perspiration and his hair glistened in the work light. Continuing in silence for the next few minutes, Herb surveyed his truck, nodded a thank you to Harry and joined the other trucks heading out for the early morning deliveries.

"Have a great trip today, Herb." Harry winked. "I mean, have a great route."

Yes, the weather was going to be hot, but it was not yet overwhelmingly warm at the unholy hour the Magic Dairy trucks hit Miry Brook Road. The humidity though. Everything was wet and although the higher temperatures were a few hours away, each driver felt sticky and uncomfortable. Wind coursing through the open door helped cool things off along with the proximity of the ice bags.

Herb completed most of his uneventful run without delay. It was a short route today because of the number of people still on vacation so he arrived at Rogers Park just after 11 a.m. He pulled up close enough to get some shade and spied the manila card. In a business-like mood and wanting to get on with it, Herb quickly grabbed the card and hopped back into his truck while everything turned white.

Adjusting to his surroundings, Herb found himself sitting in a coach car of a train passing mountains on one side and palm trees on the other. It was a curious sight for a Connecticut boy. Was he in Florida? No, there we no mountains in Florida. Must be California or perhaps Arizona. The answer came soon enough as the train passed increasingly populated areas, before long pulling into a railway station marked Los Angeles.

A few weeks earlier, in the hills near L-A at Forest Home, Billy Graham had been dealing with a crisis of faith that had begun in Altoona Pennsylvania where low turnouts and low energy at his revival meetings planted seeds of doubt as to whether he should even continue preaching. The president of a small religious college in Minnesota, Graham was struggling mightily as a few of his contemporaries challenged him on whether in fact, the Bible was the true word of God.

There was much to ponder and much to doubt as some of the stories and claims made therein seemed in a worldly sense to be nothing more than fantastic tales written by men with an agenda to push. Should he continue to preach? Should he return, defeated, to his college job and put aside what was seemingly becoming more of a pastime than a calling? He was troubled and deeply so, irritated, and sleepless. Something had to give.

Other than receiving my confirmation at the First Congregational Church, one of the things I recall vividly about my Sunday School studies was a session where our group leader,

Mrs. Watson imbued in each of us a future mission. It seemed oddly curious at the time, but she told us that we each would someday be responsible for 2,000 lives. I stored that bit of information away but had no clue what it really meant or how in the world such a responsibility would present itself or be played out.

A dozen or more years later, one night as I was performing my duties as a Coast Guardsman working in New York at the Automated Mutual-Assistance Vessel Rescue System, or AMVER, I was doing some research and going over the contents of a new instruction manual I was creating. It hit me like a thunderclap. There, in the early morning hours during a lull in the data receiving and processing, I saw that our plot of participating ships in the AMVER system was hovering right around 2,000. It was a typical number of ships on the plot in our fledgling computer system. Furthermore, it was my responsibility as a watch supervisor and now the training officer to make sure all these ships were properly coded into the system and had accurate plots on the computer so they could be called upon in a moment's notice to come to the aid of another ship somewhere in the vast ocean. Mrs. Watson had been right. How she knew to plant that future obligation with us and with that particular number, I haven't a clue, but it was a bolt of awareness that was the first thread of an intricate and painstakingly created web that would take years to draw me back to Christ.

Growing up in the church, I felt comfortable with what was being taught, and embraced the goodness of it all, if that makes sense, but hadn't gone "all in" with a prayer of salvation or a second baptism. In those times, the first baptism as a baby was pretty much accepted as being valid for life, despite the child having no awareness. I loved the fact that I was baptized so young and had the document to prove it; I was unaware that a second one, with awareness and surrender, might also be in order.

Around the time I received my driver's license (yes, on my sixteenth birthday) and discovered that dates with girls could be a most enjoyable activity, my interest in the church gave way to more worldly endeavors. Dating, cars, music. By the time I went away to college a year and a half later, the pleasures of the flesh had long since left the allure of salvation in the dust. Notwithstanding the occasional flash of awareness such as the realization I experienced at AMVER; it remained that way for forty years.

As Billy Graham dealt with his inner battle in the hills at Forest Home, one sleepless night after another, he reached an impasse. A choice simply had to be made. There was no other way. One moonlit night in the clear mountain air, he arose from the bed where he could purchase no sleep to go for a walk. The path eventually led to a tree stump where he sat to rest and solemnly came to his choice. Holding his Bible, he asserted that he was simply going to choose to believe it – every word – as the word of God. No equivocation, no doubts, and no letting others dissuade him with worldly contradictions. By faith alone, he chose to believe, and it was the most powerful event the preacher would ever personally encounter.

Coming down from that hilltop, the Billy Graham Crusade continued in Los Angeles, the so-called "flop" in Altoona quickly forgotten. An event planned for continuous nights of revival spanning a few weeks drew over-capacity crowds at the corner of Washington Street and Hill Street. An enormous tent held no less than 6,000 wooden folding chairs and a raised pulpit so everyone could see; even those on the outside. The 1949 so-called "Canvas Crusade" marked Billy Graham's exposure to the world as a fiery, fervent preacher who formulated his sermons with biblical verses; verses that to Billy were beyond reproach as the unfettered word of God. His conviction was unmistakably strong and pure, his preaching held a nearly magical hold over the total of 350,000 people who came to the tent over an extended run of eight weeks.

Herb Lundy had heard of Mr. Graham and must have read an article recently or heard the name on the radio. He had no other understanding of how this time trip was guided to Los Angeles, to this tent revival. Regardless, he was in the burgeoning California city. Stepping off the train at Union Station, he thought to buy a newspaper. It showed a date in mid-October 1949, a time with which Herb was completely familiar. The Los Angeles Examiner proclaimed the wild success of the Billy Graham religious revival, going on every night and twice on Sunday.

Crowds to that point had been truly impressive frequently overflowing to the perimeters of the huge tent. With newspaper promotion made possible by William Hearst who curiously declared to his staff, "Puff Graham," the nightly events exploded in popularity. Other newspapers around the nation quickly picked up on the remarkable story unfolding in Los Angeles securing Billy's introduction to the rest of the world as a preacher whose sermons were so powerful, whose animated delivery so convincing, that he was surely a major religious force and shooting star on the revival circuit.

Herb knew why he was in Los Angeles. It was a short cab ride from Union Station to the Canvas Crusade. With no other business at hand in the rapidly expanding city, Herb arrived in plenty of time – hours actually – to grab one of the wooden folding chairs in the front row near the pulpit; a seat location that was not lost on him as he patiently waited, reading the rest of the newspaper as the event time drew near. The crowd swelled and before Mr. Graham was announced, it had grown to become several standing rows deep beyond the tent walls. This was not your standard church service; this was people yearning for truth, for answers, and Billy Graham was going to deliver them with fire, with passion, and with fists of faith rising and falling together in time with and in tune to vital points of scripture.

Herb not so much remembered every word that Reverend Graham spoke, but he certainly remembered the nearly violent fist-pumping, the totally convicted words of scripture that flew from Billy's mouth. Billy writhed, he motioned sharply to his right and to his left, he held his Bible over his head as if Moses himself was demanding his followers see and understand the very Ten Commandments. He was an unstoppable force with the backing of immutable truths. He completely believed every bit of scripture he related to the massive crowds, and he offered no quarter to anyone or anything that might dare disagree. No man was ever so sure of his words that night, and for dozens of nights before and after the night Herb watched and listened, wondering at the pure speaking power of the man and his ability to capture the crowd.

It was either mass hysteria or masses responding to the direct word of God, so powerfully presented there was no doubting the veracity of the presenter. The only thing left to doubt was the level of acceptance by the crowd. As he did with every meeting, Billy invited to come forward anyone who was ready to accept Christ, to commit to a life in Christ and to be saved by the blood of Christ. Those who would choose that night to admit they are sinners, to ask for forgiveness of and repent of their sins, to accept that Christ is the true son of God, and to invite Christ to come into their lives were the ones Graham sought. And they came.

Billy gave his well-known invitation, one night with the same fervor as the next. "Those of you that will receive Christ, those of you who will accept Him, those of you who will trust Him," he emphasized each phrase with downward motions of his fists. "Those of you who promise you will live for Him from now on, you are receiving Him as your Lord and Savior. You're making sure that if you die, you'll go to heaven. By an act of repentance and faith, you're giving your life to Christ tonight. Those of you who will accept Him quietly and reverently, I want you to stand up where you are. If you are already standing, I want you to raise your hand and keep it there." People stood one by one, then in groups, quietly as commanded.

Hundreds, thousands of people, in fact, stood and some crowded to the pulpit, cutting off Herb's view. Those already standing, almost to a person, raised their hand. Organ music played adding drama to the moment. Billy remarked about how many were standing, encouraging more to join them. Also known as the Sinner's Prayer, Billy led the group, chanting the transitional words, telling the crowd to repeat them in their own voice, pausing to give them a chance to follow with him:

'Dear Lord Jesus ... I know that I am a sinner, and I ask for your forgiveness ... I believe you died for my sins and rose from the dead ... I turn from my sins and invite you to come into my heart and life ... I want to trust and follow you as my Lord and Savior ... In Your Name, Amen." Simple. Clean. Powerful.

Billy continued, "Now if you have said this prayer then you are now a child of Christ. Go to your church or find a church. Get a Bible and read it. Talk with your family and friends; tell them of your good news."

It was an enthralling moment, to see so many people give their lives to Christ and yet, Herb even though he was standing in front of the powerful speaker, did not, could not repeat the Sinner's Prayer. He was almost there but not completely. He felt disappointed but intrigued. More intrigued than ever before, just not enough to step through that door. Close. Close. He needed to think about it. The analytical type, he had to fight analysis with pure faith, and he knew it. Knowing so much of the ways of the world and still lacking the innocent faith of a child was perhaps the problem. Herb wanted it, yet he hesitated. In that moment, he realized there was one step missing; he needed to give his testimony to someone he knew, someone he could trust and who would help him take that fateful step. Filled now with confidence, he touched the manila card.

So many years adrift, I found myself making fun of fake preachers on TBN and using that as proof that Christianity was a fraud. If these so-called men of God were working the television for their own gain, then the whole thing must be fake. None were in the same ballpark as Billy Graham, either, As the saying might go in a sports context, none of them were worthy of holding Billy Graham's jockstrap.

Somewhere after the time my mother died, I was mockingly watching a show on TBN where fake preachers were asking for love gifts that would help burn people's debt. Call in, pledge money and tell the operator how much debt you owed. One, in particular, talked about how many billions of dollars of consumer debt there was and literally said, "If we could have had that money, we could have had Jesus back by now." Well. Proof positive in my cynical view that these guys were all charlatans. The man even went on to encourage people to call in with a credit card, forgetting to mention how that would add to the crushing consumer debt already on the books. I told and retold this ridiculous story, thinking that "they were all alike." But as time wore on, I came to a revelation of my own, though at the moment I did not recognize it.

It was November of 1988. With a long commute to work, I usually listened to a radio talk show, and most of the time it was Miami's Neal Rogers, an acerbic cynic if there ever was one. On a news break, the announcer mentioned that there were some 14,000 homeless people in South Florida and of those, the majority were children. How could that be, I thought. It seemed wildly exaggerated yet why would anyone make up such a number?

That night was supposed to herald a heavy meteor shower, so I decided to take my chances in the backyard despite the intruding city lights. It was chilly, so after a while, I went instead to get a sweater. A little while longer, and I went to get a jacket. I was still cold, and then I had something placed on my heart. I cannot explain why, but I was given the awareness that while I could easily go inside and get warm, there were those 14,000 people, my neighbors if the truth is told, who could not. It hit me like a two by four.

The next day at work, I quickly searched

for and found a local agency that helped homeless people. They were in downtown Miami. As an employee in the information technology department of a very large national bank with offices west of Miami, I had access to a sizeable group of coworkers. I literally passed a hat around the department, telling people about Camillus House, the services provided, and how many people needed help. I remember the tally; $142.10. Excited, I took my lunchtime and drove downtown, telling the receptionist I had a donation to make. There were groups of homeless men hanging around the perimeter of the property. I was introduced to Brother Harry who politely listened to my story, accepted the cash donation and told me that they could use help with business clothes, mostly for skinny underfed men, who needed something to wear to job interviews. Could I help?

Within a week, I had conducted a clothing drive in the entire seven-story building and had over a thousand pieces of clothing to take to Brother Harry. From there, I got a grant from the headquarters office for $10,000 of commercial kitchen equipment and went on to find ways to help other agencies including children's shelters. I was on a roll and had absolutely no idea why.

Over the next twenty years, I leveraged my work positions, including that of marketing director, to marshal hundreds of thousands of dollars and other donations and I still didn't know why, but it was slowly becoming evident. I was circling closer back to my faith but was still skeptical. The most prominent and frequent indication was a growing interest in my hometown of Danbury, though I'd been gone for many years. I became obsessed with knowing the latest news, of trying to find old friends, fantasizing about moving back. For a time, I even got the News-Times mailed to me. What I later realized is that I was yearning for the First Congregational Church. I wanted to go "home" but instead of just the town, it was home to my old church, and to Christ.

On February 29th, 2008, I had a meeting at His House Children's Home in Opa Locka Florida with the lady who oversaw community relations. A great organization, they encouraged businesses to come in and spruce up the properties that housed their children under care.

She wanted to know if my credit union would take on such a project. It seemed kind of overwhelming, but I agreed as the wheels began turning on how to get the money and volunteers. We chatted about my many other community activities and I related the meteor shower story and others. I told her about my nephew who was fighting Leukemia for the second time, how I was obtaining help to build a safe clean room for him and to trying to help my brother and sister-in-law deal with some of these challenges. I was moved to tears as she held out her hands across the desk and invited me to pray. She said a prayer for my nephew and then she said a prayer for me and my ministry. My ministry? What ministry? And then it sank in.

Everything good I had been doing for twenty years while living a life in a very secular world, not having given serious thought to accepting Christ, was my awkward and crooked road to my own salvation. I don't tell the story to glorify myself; to the contrary. It was simply how things played out in my case.

I was on the very edge. And the next day, relating the ministry story, I stepped through the door. I had a mental image of Jesus holding open a door for me, checking his watch. How odd. I interpreted it as him saying, "It's about time," but a good friend of mine, when I told him that said, "No, he was saying, 'Right on time.'" Everyone's time is different, and for me, it took forty years in my own desert. But I was home.

The muted canvas of my life was now exploding with color. I felt elated. I picked up a Bible for the first time in decades and read the New Testament; I read the Gospels twice, the works of Jesus in red print. I asked silently for guidance to a church. I didn't want a huge mega-church but something smaller like my church in Danbury, but it was put on my heart to go visit a nearby church that held 800 people at a time, with three services every Sunday. A mega-church. But it felt right. I was greeted as a newcomer by a smiling content face belonging to a guy named Dave. I was welcomed. No judgment, no wondering where I'd been so long away from church. Just welcomed.

Sitting back in his milk truck, with not a moment having escaped his watch, Herb pondered the trip to Los Angeles. He thought about self-control. Thinking deeply, it occurred to him that self-control was really the ability to live a life guided by the fruit of the Spirit; to show love, agape love even; to find joy in every circumstance, to be a man of peace in a world succumbing to anger. He reflected on how the Holy Spirit wanted him to embrace patience in all situations, being thoughtful before responding and when given the chance, to offer kindness often and especially when not necessarily deserved. Goodness, faithfulness, and gentleness all became markers to follow, like red channel lights guiding a ship through a storm back to harbor. All these things needed self-control; it was the key, the combining factor, the glue that held it all together. There was no other explanation.

The clinching factor, the closing sentence that made the fruit of the Spirit a very real thing and very possible to grasp was this: "Against such things, there is no law." Perfect words from the Master's own disciple. Herb contemplated all his trips and thought he was ready.

Against such things

there is no law.

Chapter Thirty-One

Despite having had enough coffee to keep him awake for the next 36 hours, Jack Lundy motioned to the waiter for a refill. The impatient waiter came over with what was left in the carafe and filled Jack's cup making sure to put his watch in front of Jack's face to emphasize the fact that the Old Oak was closing. In fact, the next to the last customers had cleared out more than twenty minutes ago while Jack and Herb had been sitting at the table for almost two hours. Jack was playing for a little more time; just a few more minutes. Sighing loudly, the waiter retreated to the corner of the door leading to the kitchen, muttering something in Italian.

"So, that's it, Jack. That's my story. I don't know if it sounds far-fetched or if you think I'm a complete idiot, but that's what happened. I'd swear to it." Herb was confessing.

"So, you were in L-A in 1949? I don't remember that." Jack was teasing.

"No, Jack, I time-traveled to 1949, and it only took an instant of actual time. But it was all so vivid; the colors, the people, even the smells."

"And the other trips? All occurring in the blink of an eye?"

"Yes, no actual clock movement. I was

there in that space and time and then when I touched the card, I instantly came back."

"OK, no, I believe you. You're a bright guy. You're level-headed, a good provider, a hard worker, a good husband. I have no reason not to believe you." Jack knew his cousin well. There is no way he would dream up such a fantasy, especially one this complex.

As a deacon in his own church in New Fairfield, Jack had heard strange stories before of how people came to Christ. Some had come still dripping in fresh sin, woefully despondent with nowhere else to turn. For others like me, they had been circling closer and closer for years, looking for reasons not to accept salvation, because it meant forsaking the many distractions and sinful pleasures of the world. But it was the truth they needed, and the truth had but one home. Jack had shepherded a good number of people into their acceptance of Christ; he was on the cusp of doing it once more, for his own cousin.

The cook was noisily cleaning the rest of the pots and pans, sending a not-too-subtle message. The waiter turned off one set of lights. Jack looked over at the waiter and held up his hand in a pleading "just one more minute" gesture, emphasizing the motion by holding up his index finger. The waiter pointed at his watch and stormed into the kitchen.

"I'm ready, Jack. I want this. I need this."

Herb's eyes were glistening. His heart was welling like an active volcano ready to explode. Jack nodded and stood up, leaning over with one hand on the red and white checkered tablecloth and the other on Herb's shoulder. From his shirt pocket, he handed Herb a well-worn card with some writing on it he'd gotten at a tent revival meeting eight years ago. It was as good a Sinner's Prayer as any other.

"Read this with me, Herb." They read aloud together.

"Dear Lord Jesus ... I know that I am a sinner, and I ask for your forgiveness ... I believe you died for my sins and rose from the dead ... I turn from my sins and invite you to come into my heart and life ... I want to trust and follow you as my Lord and Savior ... In Your Name, Amen."

With that, Herb took a shuddering breath and stood to hug his cousin, sobbing quietly into his shoulder. The noise from the kitchen had stopped. Both the cook and the waiter were watching from the serving window. The lights flickered and came back on. The back door of the kitchen blew open.

In a moment, Jack spoke softly. "Come on, Herb, I'll drive you home. Tomorrow's the first day of your new life." With that, Jack reached into his pocket and left double the normal tip on the table as he and Herb headed for the exit. Jack wasn't sure, but as he turned to the kitchen with a goodbye wave, he thought he saw a tear in the waiter's eye.

Herb felt lighter, freer. On the short drive to Victor Street, he became overwhelmed. He started talking rapid-fire to Jack. He was newly alive, reborn. He couldn't wait to tell June what happened. They burst in the door; Herb's arms held open in a "V for Victory" pose. June's smile was bright and broad.

"You did it!"

"Yes, indeed. I did." Herb picked up his wife and danced her around the living room like a rag doll. Jack just laughed.

"You did this to him!" She exclaimed to Jack. She was beyond joyous. Jack just nodded.

"No, June. He did it." June released herself from Herb's grasp. He was still smiling ear to ear. A tear formed and rolled down his cheek.

"I don't know how to describe this feeling. Well, I do." His eyes searched the room for the right words. "It's like, it's like the canvas of my life had been muted browns and greys and suddenly, it's filled with bright reds and blues; yellow, green, a colorful rainbow. June, I've never felt truly content before. I'm content. I'm confident, and don't forget; I do love you. I always will."

With that, June began to cry. Tears and hugs flowed. Herb's face was flush with color. He was excited; he was relieved. He was looking forward to what came next.

Eventually, Jack said his goodbyes and made the drive back up to New Fairfield. June made Herb a cup of tea and announced her retirement to the bedroom. It was half-past ten! Herb had to be up in just over six hours, but he took time to sip his tea and enjoy the quiet. The quiet! He banged the palms of his hands to his ears. The ringing was gone! Well, mostly. Instead of the constant buzzing noise, there was only a faint whisper. A small healing miracle or perhaps a physical release caused by a renewed temperament, the new ease in his spirit and the hearing improvement manifested by his new sense of contentment.

Finishing his tea, Herb surveyed the living room and sighed deeply. That night, he slept a dreamless sleep, free of marauding Focke-Wulfs and B-24s spinning out of control down to the patchwork of fields below.

Chapter Thirty-Two

Wednesday evening and the supper dishes had been cleared, washed, dried and put away. Herb sat down with the afternoon paper with a cup of tea June prepared for him. He was finally content, at home with his faith, comfortable in his new awareness and ready to reach out to share his news, but how?

A gentle knock at the door announced an unexpected visitor. June and Herb looked at each other quizzically as June dried her hands on her apron and opened the door. A slight, gentle man with longish hair, welcoming eyes and a casual demeanor stood in the doorway. June knew who it was without asking. A tender smile came over her face, matching the look on his. She gestured him inside without saying a word.

Herb looked up, then stood up, a broad smile finding its way to his face. He felt light as a feather, crossing the living room in two steps, wanting to embrace the man but not wanting to overstep his place. No matter, the man embraced him and warmly shook June's hand. Motioning to the couch, Herb waited for the man to sit and then sat next to, but not too close to him. June offered a cup of tea which the man declined.

"I've come to see how you're doing," said

the gentle visitor, already knowing the answer. Herb could barely believe he was speaking with the Lord, his Father, and Savior, in his own living room! He stammered and struggled to provide a lucid answer.

"I just want to thank you for giving me this opportunity," said Herb. "I learned so much yet at the same time, it almost seemed like I already knew these things; I just had to uncover them or something." The man nodded and said Herb was being very perceptive.

"So, I could have discovered these truths on my own?" Herb wondered.

"You could have eventually, but faith being sometimes fragile, you could just as easily have looked the other way. I thought you were one who needed to take this trip, to go full circle and come to realize for yourself the simple lessons I wanted you to know; that I want everyone to know."

Herb nodded. It made sense. Like Dorothy clicking her heels back to Kansas, it was within him all along but needed to be awakened.

"I am truly thankful for what you let me discover," Herb solemnly added. "We both are." The conversation paused.

"But, that's not the end, is it? There's something more." Herb knew inside this wasn't the end of anything, but the beginning of something new.

"How would you both like to take a trip?"

June slowly sat down. Her eyes met Herb's, then she looked at the man on the couch. She turned her head slightly, not quite understanding the offer.

"You can go together on a trip but it's a one-way journey, something that requires your total commitment. A leap of faith if you will."

June sat back in the chair, arms at her side. Herb leaned over from his place on the couch and grasped her forearm. June looked around the room, around her house. Then she looked back at the man.

"Where would we go? How ... when would we go?"

"To a time and place where you are needed; both of you. I need you in 2019. That's all I can really tell you. Do you possess the faith to do it?"

June looked at Herb as a slight smile crossed her lips. 2019? More than sixty years from now. She bobbed her head a little back and forth as if saying, "Why not?" They both stood up.

"We'll go."

A thousand questions immediately came to mind. What about the house? What about Herb's job? What would they say to their relatives and friends? The man motioned with both arms for them to sit with a reassuring nod.

"Those are not your problems. Your home

will go to good use. Yes, your friends and family will miss you but what they will know is that you both went on to a much better place. Don't get lost in the details for they are of a minor consequence." He glanced at Herb and June with a questioning look. They both sighed. June squeezed Herb's hand.

"Yes. Yes, we're OK. We'll go."

"Herb, tomorrow's Thursday. You'll have the truck. Run your regular route. Don't tell anyone that you're leaving. Harry will know what to do."

Herb's eyebrows raised up. Harry, huh? He's been in on it all along, just as Herb thought. He looked curiously at the man.

"The sooner the better. You can do this." Herb nodded. He knew the man was right.

"June, you drive to work with Herb and drop him off, then come home and wait. There will be some papers here for you. Bring them with you to the park. You can call your family and friends but just casually. No details."

"Yes, of course." June didn't know what she would say anyway – we're going somewhere in a time machine?

"Herb, finish your route by 1 p.m. then go to the tree. June, meet him there. You'll find that there is a small gold plate under the hood of your car. Herb, you know how it works. Find the card, then get in the car with June."

Chapter Thirty-Three

It was past 2 p.m. and Harry "Bucko" Stevens should have left for the day a while ago, but he was worried. Herb had not yet returned from his route. If he was anything, Herb was punctual. Maybe today was the day. He waved goodbye to the few drivers still unloading their trucks and got in his car. He headed over to Rogers Park.

Just before 1 p.m., Herb pulled up under the elm tree at Rogers Park and the Divco chugged to a stop. He killed the motor and took a deep breath. The sky he noticed, was especially blue. A warm breeze sauntered leisurely down the hillside and wove its way through his truck bringing earthy smells with it. Nothing was very distinct although a slight odor of someone burning leaves was evident. Herb glanced over at the elm and saw the card. Wandering over to the stately tree, Herb thought about what he'd heard: "I need you in 2019." This would mark the first trip where Herb knew when he was going.

The fact that he and June were not coming back was naturally concerning. People like familiarity; they like routines. He'd miss his dad of course but the few other relatives would be fine including Marcy whom he hadn't enjoyed much contact with since his high school days.

What upset him the most was leaving Stan behind. Buddies since childhood, it didn't seem fair to just up and leave. Herb thought about swinging by the bakeshop to say his goodbyes but knew it would only complicate the day and he was told not to say anything to anyone. He suspected eventually, that Stan would be OK with it; that he'd have a drink or a plate of lasagna at the Old Oak and while not knowing exactly what happened, could in good cheer raise a toast to Herb and June Lundy. Herb convinced himself of it, anyway.

People would mourn his disappearance for a bit and then move on. The Reverend Waller would notice the empty pew in the front row and ponder what had happened. June's family was much the same; no parents alive, a brother in Boston that she saw once a year. Herb took the card in his hand and sighed deeply, closing his eyes for a moment. He heard tires thumping on the rough pavement. June drove up.

"I see you found the place," Herb joked walking over to the driver's window. He was suddenly in a jovial mood. What was about to happen could not be anything to fear; it had to be something wonderful, magical; a new beginning, the opportunity of a lifetime. Two lifetimes.

"I brought a picnic basket just in case," remarked June, tapping a wicker basket on the seat. June smiled broadly and looked at the Divco truck. To her, it looked like all the others. Herb showed her the little gold plate under the hood then fumbling for the hood latch on the Ford, propped it up and saw an identical gold plate recently attached to his own car.

"That's it, huh? That's the thingamabob that will take us into the future?" June looked on skeptically.

"Well, if it doesn't actually transport us, it must have something to do with it. I expect it's some kind of power or energy that is obviously beyond our comprehension." They both looked around. It was a lovely afternoon. Birds were singing. Only faint sounds of traffic could be heard. Herb looked at June and raised his eyebrows in question. She looked over at the pond then back at Herb and just nodded. June climbed into the passenger side and Herb got in behind the wheel, the small manila card in his hand. He closed the door, and everything became white.

Harry Stevens thought he saw a car parked next to the Divco truck near the pond as he worked his way down Memorial Drive. He saw it, blinked, and then he didn't see it. Pulling up alongside the Divco, Harry got out and looked at the dirt ground. Fresh tire tracks; there had been a car here just now. He figured it was Herb's car and that he and June were now sometime else. After all, it had been Harry who'd attached the gold plate to Herb's car just yesterday. Looking into the Divco, he saw the key still in the ignition and Herb's worn copy of *The Time Machine* on the driver's seat. There was a note inside that said simply, "I know it was you." Herb also left the plain manila envelope June had brought as she had been instructed, containing the notarized quitclaim deed to the house on Victor Street along with a notice of satisfaction of the mortgage. The First Congregational Church had been named the new property owner.

Harry tucked the note into his pocket and tossed the envelope on his front seat, his work done. Satisfied, he propped open the hood of the Divco and with the special tool he'd been given, pried the small gold plate from the inside of the truck's hood. It was heavy; heavier than gold in fact. Looking around, Harry reached back like Whitey Ford winding up for a fastball and hurled the little plate into the middle of the pond.

Taking the key from the Divco and closing its doors, Harry stepped back into his own car. The Divco, ordinary now, could wait to be retrieved. His work complete, it was time to head over to Ives Street for a shot and a beer courtesy of one "Stache" Waller. He'd be eager to hear the news about his good friend.

Chapter Thirty-Four

It was the sound that startled Herb and June. They could hear trumpets and drums and clarinets all playing different tunes at once. It was a maddening sound and quite unpleasant.

Their eyes coming into focus, they could see it was a marching band practicing, individual musicians warming up. The band was positioned on a green field somewhere with a huge parking garage behind them. Harry looked around and saw nothing familiar. There was a 1957 Chevy parked in front of their '54 Ford and what looked like a 1932 Ford sedan behind them. Other cars were lined up as well. He got out.

Beyond the band, and it looked like the Danbury Drum Corps, he saw a few very sleek looking firetrucks, like nothing he'd ever imagined before. He thought he saw scout troops too, and a series of ultra-modern looking pickup trucks with displays mounted in their beds. The displays looked like things he'd seen at the Danbury Fair - little Dutch figures, a reindeer, a large cow statue of some sort.

"June, get out and look at this." June carefully opened her door and stepped out.

"Herb, I think this is a parade. Or, it's going to be one. This looks like how the

Memorial Day Parade forms up over on Rose Street. You remember."

Herb thought a bit and agreed. Firetrucks, scouts, floats, bands. They were about to be in a parade, but why?

An old man was shuffling his way from one car to the next, handing out a form to each driver. He wore a blue windbreaker and ball cap with writing on it that Herb could not make out. Eventually, he reached Herb and June. The man had some sort of pass or ticket in a clear plastic holder hanging around his neck on a lanyard. His worn-out, greasy hat declared, "Magic Dairy" in an old-time font. The pass said, "REMEMBERING DANBURY FAIR" and his name, H. Stevens. The old man winked at Herb.

Herb's jaw just dropped. "Harry, is that you?" Herb instantly realized how ridiculous it sounded. The old man just smiled.

"How have you been, Herb? Long time no see. You don't look a day older, either." Harry chuckled at his own joke. "What's it been? Oh, let's see now ... sixty-two years!" Herb quickly did the math.

"We're in 2019?" They had made it.

"Never could fool you with a math problem, Herb, unless it was Calculus. Yes, indeed, 2019, and as you can see, I'm still around." Herb reached for Harry and they embraced for a good twenty seconds. A tear came to Harry's eye. Herb's too. June walked over from around the side of the car and gently kissed Harry on the cheek.

"What are you doing here?" June asked.

"Oh, I'm just volunteering with this parade. It's in remembrance of the Danbury Fair. You wouldn't know this, but it's been shut down since 1981."

Herb shook his head. How in the world could such a wonderful fair have come to an end? Harry knew what Herb was wondering.

"Old man Leahy passed away about forty-five years ago. After that, things just started falling apart and the trustees ended up selling the fair and the property to some developer. Offers for the property kept going up and up and they finally gave in. Do you know, those people" – he nearly spit out the words – "put up a damned shopping mall. Called it the Danbury Fair Mall."

"The racetrack closed too?"

"Yup. It all got auctioned off, every bit of it. But slowly, some pieces of it have been coming back home and in fact, when this parade starts, you're going to be in for a big surprise."

"What's that?"

"Oh, just hold on. You'll see. Heck, folks around here haven't forgotten the fair. In fact, there's a bunch of memorabilia on eBay and several FaceBook pages and groups." Herb looked at Harry like he had three eyes. What in the world were eBay and FaceBook?

"Here, take one of these flyers. It's got the parade route on it and we'll all end up at Rogers Park. You know where that is." Harry winked again. "I gotta hand out the rest of these but I'll see you there."

Herb looked for a newspaper box. There were none. The man in the '32 Ford behind him had one of those transistor radio-looking things held up to his ear.

"Excuse me. What's today? Sorry, I'm a bit confused. Long trip."

"It's Saturday. You know, October 12th, when the fair would have been open." Herb hesitated to ask but did anyway.

"It is 2019, right?" The man stopped talking into his little radio.

"Yes," he said slowly and patiently. It is in fact 2019. Like your outfit by the way. Very period." Herb looked at his clothes. They were much different from what the man in the very old Ford was wearing. He walked back to June.

"Well, Harry was right. It's October 12 and the year is 2019. We're in a parade." Herb shook his head slowly and got back in the car.

"Nice car by the way!" The man in the '32 yelled out his window. It looks totally like a survivor. Original paint?" Herb nodded. Yes, in fact, it was the original paint on his three-year-old car. Or was it a sixty-five-year-old car.

The band started to form up. There were a few bands in fact. Herb guessed the one in white uniforms was the Danbury Drum Corps, and then probably the high school band was included in their orange and blue colors, and maybe the Connecticut Rebels fife and drum corps. He was guessing. June looked at the parade map. It showed the classic cars in behind a firetruck pumper from Miry Brook.

"I guess we're in a classic car now," June remarked. This could be fun. She checked the picnic basket. It had made the trip and the food looked OK. She handed Herb a sandwich. "Welcome to 2019!"

Presently, the first group moved out – a very sleek looking black convertible with someone sitting on top of the back seat. Probably the mayor, whoever that was. Preceding the car was a small group of scouts it seemed, carrying a banner. Following the black convertible came one of the floats. It was hard to see because Herb and June were parked along Ives Street just south of White Street and these buildings blocked most of their view, a view that was somewhat dominated by a huge parking garage in the background.

Bands began to play. First to leave was the Danbury Drum Corps, moving at first just to a steady drumbeat, then breaking into song as they turned out from National Place to White Street, heading east. The sound, especially the drums, echoed off the buildings. Herb thought they were playing "Under the Double Eagle." More scouts and waving politicians and city leaders followed. The unmistakable shape of the Danbury Fair Bandwagon came next and a lively small orchestra began playing a Polka. Herb did not know if it was the original bandwagon or a reproduction, but little did it matter.

In a moment, the classic cars were started. Herb turned the key on the Ford. The '32 behind them was some kind of a hot rod with a loud exhaust report and the driver did not hesitate to show it off. Before it was their turn to form up in line, Herb noticed Harry huffing along in the rear-view mirror. He was waving his hand.

"You don't mind if I ride along with you, do you? All these years, and I've never actually been in a parade."

"Of course!" Herb was thrilled. June opened up the front passenger door and got out.

"Harry, sit up front."

"Oh, it's no bother."

"No, Harry. I insist. You and Herb have a lot to talk about."

The parade continued to form up and head out. Most of the walkers had gathered on the unfamiliar green space. A sign proclaimed it to be Ives Concert Park. Herb was quite sure there would be a lot of changes to the Danbury he'd just left – the Danbury of 1957. After a few moments, the long snaking parade caught up the fire departments as the big shiny machines rolled out into place. Herb did see one that looked familiar. It was a 1955 GMC Pumper and it looked brand new. In gold lettering, the name of the company was proudly displayed; Germantown Volunteer – Danbury. The others though were all super-modern, like ones he'd seen foretold in a Popular Mechanics magazine back at the dairy. What had the man back on Garfield Avenue told him?

As if Harry could read Herb's mind, and who's to say he couldn't, he said, "Magic's been closed for years, Herb. Frank's wife passed away in 1987 and he just lost all interest in the dairy. Sold it to Marcus and from what I know, didn't even negotiate. Sad." Yes, Herb remembered now; it was indeed sad.

Harry continued, "But the Marcus family sold the property on Sugar Hollow Road about ten years ago. Said the real estate was worth more than milk and a shopping center went in. The Marcus Dairy silo is still there but no dairy bar or dairy. They tried to outsource milk production for a while but ended up closing down the entire operation a few years ago."

Herb sighed. He well knew that change is inevitable and that in the end, money talks.

The parade was now in full motion. The classic cars were the last element other than one of the old Danbury Fair horse-drawn wagons bringing up the rear. This was fun! As the line of cars turned on to White Street, Herb couldn't believe his eyes. There were hundreds, if not thousands of people celebrating this parade, this nostalgic and loving look back at their beloved fair. Among the crowd, he saw plenty of young people, too young to have ever visited the fair, but excited, all the same, having been told of it by their parents and grandparents and watching old home movies on a station called YouTube. Herb caught a glimpse of some of the artifacts turning right at an unfamiliar corner just before the railway station. And then he saw it. The big kahuna. Uncle Sam, himself.

"Wow!" It was all Herb could muster. He looked at Harry who had a big grin on his face.

"Told ya."

"June, look at that!" Herb pointed out the window at the gleaming red, white and blue figure, newly painted and standing proudly at the corner of White Street and some new street called Patriot Drive. A grandstand had been put up in the parking lot of the railway station, now a museum Herb noted, and parade-goers lined both sides of the street, waving, clapping and laughing; jumping for joy even, just as if they had been let out of school for a free day at the fair itself. Wonder of wonders.

Uncle Sam stood at least thirty-five feet

tall; taller even, if Herb could judge the height. He held a cane in his left hand and was grasping at air with his right. Had he ever held anything in that big hand? Herb stopped the Ford to ponder and wonder. June wore the smile of a child on Christmas morning. Harry just chuckled. Beep! The '32 behind Herb urged him to move ahead and catch up, the driver waving Herb forward. This was a parade after all, not a parking lot.

The parade motored slowly down this unfamiliar road called Patriot Drive. There were a number of new buildings casting shadows across the smooth street. Crowds lined up three and four-deep were clapping and waving, pointing to Herb's car and calling his name. Calling his name? How could that be? Harry seemed to know what Herb was thinking.

"I'll explain later." Reach down and feel alongside the door. Herb did so and felt some kind of panel; a sign maybe. He wondered what it could be.

After a few minutes, the parade turned right onto Liberty Street. Aha! A street name that was familiar. Herb knew the parade was heading towards Main Street and he was right. Following the Miry Brook firetruck and its annoying siren, Herb pointed the Ford south onto Main Street. This was more like it. The stone facades and brick buildings welcomed him. The Civil War statue of a Union Army soldier still guarded the entrance to the gently upsloping West Street. Herb saw a brick building and a sign that said Danbury Library. He looked at Harry.

"This library was built about oh, forty-five years ago. Had a big fire back in 1996 but they restored it." June pointed out the fact that cars were parked parallel to the sidewalk now, not at an angle like back in 1957.

On the left June spotted the Palace Theater. It had a modern awning and the marquee did not indicate any movies were playing but there were some musical groups listed, or at least that's what she thought those names meant. But where was the Empress? She tapped Harry on the shoulder.

"You're wondering about the Empress Theater, right? Well, that closed back in 1969. Turned it into an office building or something and it changed hands a couple of times."

As a child and into my teen years, I was a frequent visitor to both the Palace and Empress theaters. For pocket change, we'd file in, buy some candy or popcorn and sit through some cartoons and a double feature ... it was an afternoon out. I vividly remember cheering on Westerns, trembling to The Blob and seeing my first James Bond thriller. It was not a long walk from my home; my great aunt called that walk to Main Street, "going up-street."

My friend Randy who lived on Deer Hill Avenue was from a family that supposedly owned the entire block where the theaters were located. He and I and his little brother on several occasions would go to the movies and he'd simply tell the ticket taker his last name and we were automatically admitted. On one occasion, the last name failed to impress the theater employee. Randy said, "We OWN the building." After considering the situation for about a half-second, the usher let us in. Randy enjoyed the celebrity of it; I felt like we were getting away with something.

June noticed and mentioned the narrow grass median that now divided this section of Main Street adding a bit of charm to an already charming artery. As the parade chugged along, still with Danbury Fair fans lined up three deep, Herb pointed out the building that last time he knew was the Brass Rail except it was now something called a Churrascaria. Dominating their view, however, was the grand St. Peter's Church rising above nearby buildings just as it had yesterday, or sixty-two years ago. It was comforting to see the wonderful edifice still overseeing Danbury's Main Street.

My mother's funeral service was held at St. Peter's in the late summer of 1999. Even though we grew up in the Congregational Church, after she remarried following my dad's untimely and early death eighteen years before, she converted to Catholicism which pleased her new husband immensely and gave her a wonderful foundation of faith through her remaining years. That emotional service was the first and only time I'd ever been inside St. Peter's.

Herb and June were both delighted to see that Elmwood Park, the larger median that was kind of a signature space on the southern part of Main Street was not only intact but beautifully maintained. Herb looked over at the building where the Main Street Bake Shop had been; now a Chinese restaurant, and sighing, thought of his friend Stan. They passed the impressive and somewhat gothic looking buildings of St. Peter School and the rectory, and where Herb had last seen the Dan-Ridge Chevy dealership, there now stood a more modern building that housed a health care center. The street had changed so much while parts of it remained exactly the same.

Harry broke the silence. "Just a bit different, don't ya think?"

"It's very different in some ways but so familiar in others," Herb replied. "It's like I know exactly where I am but at the same time, I'm kind of lost." People were still lined up and waving and so June continued to wave out the back window and Harry waved too, often to welcoming cheers. The general enthusiasm of a parade honoring the long-closed fair or something more like a hero's welcome?

They were approaching South Street and

the mix of buildings was more diverse; a lot of newer buildings without much character mingled with older buildings which had been there since before Herb was a boy. The old Grand Union store set back from Main Street was now something called a Price Rite. The wide-open intersection at South Street was familiar in shape and dimension only. An urgent care center occupied one corner and Herb thought it must be a miniature hospital. The Rogers Park Pharmacy was apparently long gone replaced by a big parking lot and something called CVS. The gas station on the wide sweeping turn was now a muffler shop but the familiar War Memorial had not been displaced, though there were a few new monuments including one up near the street for something called the Vietnam War.

Harry chimed in. "There was a terrible war Herb. We lost more than 50,000 servicemen in the '60s and '70s and damned if we didn't run from it at the end with our tail between our legs. Can you believe it? And some soldiers came back from that war and got spit at and swore at for being baby killers. It's a long and sad story. I don't even want to talk about it." Harry turned his head away from the monument, wishing it did not need to exist and sorry for the loss of the young men from Danbury and elsewhere.

While my service did not include time in Vietnam, we lost two guys from our immediate neighborhood in the early part of the conflict. They grew up just a few blocks from each other. Larry Visconti, the older brother of one of our neighborhood group was first, in 1967. It was a kick-in-the-gut moment and a cold dose of reality for those of us a few years from draft age. In 1970, our neighbor from Grand Street, Richard Hope, son of the man who would eventually become my stepfather, lost his life. Two lives gone among many others from Western Connecticut, all of their names permanently and lovingly etched on a black stone memorial in the nation's capital. Among them were names such as Flynn, Goetz, Baker, Benicewicz, Bickford, Kelly, McCarthy, Repole, Zaborowski, and many more. Each one fondly remembered.

Continuing down Memorial Drive the crowds of onlookers came to an end as did the parade. Being at the end of the parade, we learned most of the other participants had packed up and left but a few of the relics from the fair were still there, mounted on pickup trucks or trailers. They looked completely familiar to Herb and June, including the Ringmaster with his top hat, a couple of figures from Stuyvesant's Court, a few artifacts from the Blacksmith Shop, a large flying goose, and a trailer with a restored racecar number 151. If something was not familiar to them, it was at least typical of the hundreds of display items for which the fair was so well known and for so many years.

"It's so sad the fair had to end," June said wistfully, surveying the artifacts.

"People are still sore about it, and what's it been? Thirty-eight years?" Harry was one of those who still mourned the passing of the fair. With the resigned voice of one who no longer chose to deny defeat, he mumbled, "Well, what are you gonna do?"

"I can still hear the sound of those racecars echoing all the way down here at Rogers Park." Herb half-closed his eyes remembering the guttural sounds of the Ford flathead eight-cylinder engines. It was more vivid up close and personal but those days apparently and sadly, were long gone.

"What did you say earlier, Harry ... something about Danbury Fair information being available on ...?"

"On FaceBook," Harry replied. "It's an online thing where friends get together and share stories and pictures and stuff." Harry on purpose didn't explain any of it.

"Online? What does online mean?" Herb was totally confused.

"It's on the computer. The PC." Harry sighed. Herb and June certainly had a lot of catching up to do.

"Well, I've heard of a computer but that's like something the government owns, right? It's the size of a whole room." Herb tried to comprehend.

"Well, yeah but over the years, they became much smaller and people started having them in their homes. Heck, a smartphone is a computer when you come down to it." Harry knew he was taking Herb for a ride but enjoyed every moment.

"Now the smartphone; is that what everyone is holding up to their heads?"

"Yeah, that's right. Here, look at mine." He offered his Samsung Galaxy for Herb to look at. June leaned forward over the back seat. The little device had a tiny color TV screen on it that had little odd symbols that could be pressed to make different things happen.

"What's this symbol for?" Herb pointed to a little orange box that had an open quote shape.

"That's to send text messages instead of speaking to someone. That's how most of the kids communicate with each other." Herb just shrugged and handed the smartphone back.

"People don't call each other these days?"

"Well sure, see this little green symbol with the phone graphic? That's how you call someone." Herb made a surrender gesture with his hands. "And no, there are no wires."

"June, I think we've got a lot of catching up to do."

Chapter Thirty-Five

The post-parade participants had mostly left the park. It was time for Herb and June to go somewhere, but where?

"Harry, can we drive you somewhere?" Herb sure didn't think it was fair for Harry to have to walk a mile back to the parade starting location on Ives Street. It made him wonder how he got there in the first place.

"Well, how do you feel about me showing you around just a bit more? Then you can drop me at my apartment."

"Sure. You didn't drive to the start of the parade, did you?" Herb kind of shuddered at the thought of this old man driving around town.

"Heck no. I took an Uber."

Herb slowly turned to look at June and she did the same, eyebrows raised. Uber?

"Hey, let's stop in here at the CVS. I just got an email saying my prescription is ready for pickup." Email? Herb did a three-point turn near where the rose trellises were supposed to be, but there was a parking lot instead. He pulled into the entrance at the CVS Pharmacy.

"Take one of the handicapped spots," said Harry, pointing them out to a confused Herb. "Here, stick this in your window so we don't get in trouble." Harry pulled a small placard out of his jacket pocket. It showed a stick figure of a person in a wheelchair and had the words, "Expires - Lifetime" printed. But Harry didn't use a wheelchair. They all got out to go see what a pharmacy in 2019 looked like. It was a shock to the senses.

While Harry ambled his way to the back of the huge store, Herb and June strolled up and down the many aisles of products, marveling at the prices. It was much more than a pharmacy; it was a department store and a grocery store, too.

"Look at this!" June pointed to a two-pack of Dial bar soap. "That should be no more than 25 cents!" The label on the shelf showed $3.29! It was a three-pack, not a regular two-pack, but still.

"Here's another one!" June was starting to sweat. "This toilet tissue is $4.29! I just paid 90 cents for eight rolls the other day!" She glanced around the store at some of the other items then grabbed Herb by the sleeve. "How are we going to afford to live here?"

"There's sure a lot of choices, I can tell you that much." Herb was amazed at just how many ways there were to buy simple things like toothpaste. And the brand names! Some were familiar, like Colgate and others quite strange, like Sensodyne. He just shook his head. Instead of just aspirin, the store featured half a row of nothing but pain relievers. Something called ibuprofen and something else called acetaminophen. And yes, good old Bayer aspirin. Some of the prices seemed phenomenally high. So many ways to calm a headache or achy joints, all at a princely sum. Harry slowly walked up, a slight limp to his right leg.

"Got what I needed," he said, holding up his bag. Herb thought to ask how much prescriptions must cost these days but hesitated.

"Looks like you two are suffering from sticker shock." A blank look. "You know, the cost of things now compared to 1957."

"Yes. Yes, we are in – sticker shock. I mean, how can you afford to live? How do you afford your medication?" June pointed towards the clear plastic bag stuffed with paperwork.

"Oh, my Part D covers that."

"Part D? Part D of what?"

"You know. Medicare." More blank looks. Harry turned his eyes skyward, thinking.

"Oh yeah. Medicare didn't come around until 1965. It's health insurance for old people like me. And you both, if you'd a stuck around." Harry laughed at his own joke. "OK, let's go." Harry led Herb and June out of the CVS, waving to the Indonesian-looking clerk at the front counter on the way out.

Going back to the car, Herb noticed the sign for the first time; the one attached to the car that Harry spoke of and Herb forgot amidst all the strange sights they'd seen. It was a magnetic sign, about 18 by 24 inches. "Lundy Life Skills – Coming Soon," and in smaller lettering, "First Congregational Church, Danbury." Harry saw Herb studying the sign.

"About that. You know how you were told you were needed in 2019?" Herb looked and June. They both nodded. "Well, that's what it's about. Let's head up to the church."

Chapter Thirty-Six

Herb turned west on South Street. No
more Studebaker dealership. The space was now
part of the huge CVS parking lot. Across the
street was that urgent care center next to a
Dunkin' Donuts. Have a donut, have a heart
attack, go right next door to get fixed. Handy.
The rest of the street looked unchanged, most of
the homes surviving the decades.

Herb turned the old Ford left on to
Mountainville Road, then sharply right to Seeley
Street. He noticed the vacant lot at the corner, the
familiar enclosed porch on the side of the old
Tartaglia home, the white farm-rail fence
surrounding the Smith property, and yes, the lot
next to the old Constantini home at the corner of
Housman was still strangely vacant. Most of the
homes had been updated with siding or fancy
brick driveways but oh, the street was a welcome
sight. What he did not see was a single home that
had a galvanized milk box on the front porch.
Herb downshifted to match the gravity demands
of the increasingly steep hill, stopping at the
corner of Deer Hill Avenue just momentarily, so
he didn't have to fully release the clutch. They
drove along Deer Hill Avenue, the stately homes
nearly unchanged over so many years. It was still

a lovely old avenue, maple and chestnut trees along the curb, oversized lots with houses that were already well-established when Herb was a boy. A traffic light at Wooster Street kept vehicles moving in an orderly fashion and Herb recalled that the ancient Garfield Elm was just a block or so away. Continuing towards West Street, Herb noted the former home of his old boss, Frank Mark. He'd been there a few times for Christmas parties, and once when Frank had a special favor to ask of Herb, a favor whose details or purpose he could not recall.

Some of the trees were ablaze with fall colors and leaves cluttered the curbsides. There was an unfamiliar property called Deer Hill Arms. Frank was curious.

"What's that place?"

"Herb, that's a condominium."

"A condo-what?"

"It's like an apartment but you buy it with a mortgage and everything. You share common expenses." Herb vaguely remembered reading about condominiums in some forgotten journal but to his knowledge, he'd never seen one.

A series of old homes seemed to have been converted to business offices and law firms. Momentarily, they arrived at city hall on the right and the unmistakable visage of the First Congregational Church on the left with its gleaming white columns and gold cupola that soared to the blue New England sky. Four clocks, one on each face of the tower that to this day showed the correct time. Herb pulled into the small paved parking lot that noted the presence of a thrift shop along with the church. For some reason, it occurred to Herb that in the many trips on Deer Hill Avenue, he'd never seen a deer.

"Let's go inside. I want to show you folks to your new office."

Chapter Thirty-Seven

Like Richard Nixon, I grew up in the house my father built, but the similarities ended right there. My father, far from being tricky was quite skilled in a variety of ways, including carpentry and general construction owing to his education at Henry Abbot Technical School.

Until about age six, my mom and dad, older sister Jan and I lived with my grandparents in a stately, two-story home, three if you count the finished attic, built in 1879 on the corner of Grand Street and South Street. My grandparents and great aunt lived upstairs on the second floor while the four of us lived on the main floor. While a little cramped, it was very workable and comfortable until the news came that my mom was expecting twins. Something had to give.

A vacant lot on nearby Seeley Street adjacent to my grandparent's property was for sale and my dad made the leap. Using blueprints for a modest Cape Cod style home he bought from a catalog, he got to work as the main builder and self-contractor. He hired someone to dig out the foundation on the hilly lot, and they put in the footings and a basement slab and built the high walls from concrete blocks, each block meticulously leveled and cemented into place.

I only recall seeing the foundation once, as the waterproofing material was applied before the land was filled in. A young boy has little value or interest in the construction of a home, but I did manage to find a board with a nail sticking out from it and promptly fell on it, butt-first. The pain was – unique – and fortunately, the nail did not impact anything vital. Still, it was a lesson learned and retained to this day.

The building progressed over months, my dad intimately involved with every joist, every nail, every length of electrical conduit and plumbing pipe. He hired laborers and carpenters to help where needed but he directed every interior wall to its rightful place, every door leveled to its frame. It was a masterful job and one for which I had no appreciation at such a tender age.

The front of the home had a rather steep slope from the top of the second floor to the front door. A carefully constructed brick chimney rose from the downhill side of the building and the basement wall rose several feet above ground here where in contrast, it was fully buried on the uphill side. It was a fine house with three bedrooms and two bathrooms. Not spacious especially by today's standards but enough for the six of us, even if it meant me sharing a small bedroom jammed with three beds for me and my twin brothers. The steep slope of the roofline created several oddly configured void spaces to which my dad had added access doors. For all I know, there may still be a dusty box of old baseball cards in that secret space.

My sister had her own room on the other side of the second floor and I was continually jealous. Baby pictures of her adorned the walls of our home in gold-edged frames while the earliest photo of me was when I was perhaps two, getting a haircut from my great aunt. The plight of the middle child.

In the totality of my life, the few years spent on Seeley Street were among the brief best. The neighborhood kids would hang out constantly and we'd range far and wide without the overseeing gaze of our parents. It was assumed we were having fun outside somewhere and further assumed that our stomachs would bring us home in time for dinner. The notion of a helicopter parent was decades from forming. Milk bottles appeared on our front porch in a galvanized box and the egg lady stopped by every so often with farm-fresh eggs. There was no dragging of garbage cans down to the curb; the burly garbageman would hoist the metal can to his shoulder and carry it out to the truck.

In the spring, we'd ride home-made go-carts dangerously down Seeley Street, and, in the winter, our sleds would just as dangerously fly down the icy hill. No memorable injuries occurred despite our reckless ways. As I grew older, summers meant earning some money mowing lawns or caddying over at Rock Ridge Country Club. Other than one more summer spent at home between college semesters and weekends off and on before I left for boot camp, these were among my last days living on Seeley Street. While I was away doing Coast Guard things, my parents moved to a larger home on more land out on Grammar School Drive, something of a stately looking property with the home set back well away from the street. With my formative years spent on Seeley Street, even as a young adult, it was a shock to the system.

My Coast Guard career eventually took me south to Florida and I liked it. I didn't get home to Danbury much at all and anyway, their new home was no longer where I grew up. Later, my parents moved to a condo off Padanaram Road, a pleasant but nondescript home that was completely unfamiliar to me. Not long after, my dad passed away in his sleep at age 58, taken many years too early, canceling my plans to grow closer to the man as he achieved retirement including a move to St. Augustine.

With that nostalgia living within me for decades, it came to me eventually that as I grew tired of defending against hurricane seasons and months on end of humidity and heat, that a move back north might be in order. I was of retirement age although for the life of me, I don't know what I would do with myself if I didn't stay busy. I knew of several old chums who had done the same, ventured across the country in their earning years only to relocate back to Danbury later in life. A trip to visit my parents' gravesites in early 2017 then led me to come to what the Wizard of Oz called a cataclysmic decision; I would move back to Danbury.

The town was enormously different than when I came of age, but plenty was still familiar including Rogers Park, Candlewood Lake, and the familiar dog-face rock. Decades-old statues and monuments, plus newer ones adorned the corner of West Street and Main and at the War Memorial. I could even get a JK's Texas Hot Weiner. Along with missing changes in seasons, it was lovely enough to make my decision a fait accompli.

Cruising along in my old neighborhood, I simply had to stop at my old home on Seeley Street. It had changed, of course, there was a small entry room at the front door now, a fence along the property line, and what appeared to be a sunroom in the backyard. Being a bit bold, I pulled into the driveway and went to knock on the door. I was greeted with an inquisitive smiling face, its owner wondering why some old guy was knocking on her door.

"Please excuse me for intruding," I

explained, "I grew up here. My father built this house and I just couldn't help stopping by." The owner gave me a skeptical look.

"I'm quite serious. My bedroom was up the stairs to the right. I helped my dad build the concrete patio slab one summer."

"Oh, that's where our sunroom is now," she replied. "My name is Martha. Would you like to come in?" Martha was trusting enough to open her door to an unannounced stranger.

I introduced myself in return. "Yes, if it's not too much trouble. I won't take up much of your time."

"Not at all. Do you still live in Danbury?" She waved me inside, holding open the screen door leading to the small entryway.

"No, I haven't lived here for many years. In fact, when I joined the Coast Guard, I left this house for the last time and when I was able to come home on leave, my parents had moved."

"My nephew is in the Coast Guard! What a small world." We chatted about the old Coast Guard I knew and the new one in which the nephew was serving. I told her that many of the things we got away with back then would be grounds for dismissal today. I offered to send her an autographed copy of my Coast Guard book.

The home was tiny inside, at least in comparison to my memory. Upon entering, there was a small closet to the left, then a door to the master bedroom. Directly in front of the front door was the stairway leading to the upstairs bedrooms and bathroom. My younger twin brothers had slid down those stairs bouncing on their butts many times wearing out their corduroy pants to my mom's dismay.

The living room picture window through which I had watched the snow falling in the streetlight was now a bowed bay window with a small seating area and the wood paneling that had adorned the wall with the unchanged fireplace had long since been replaced. My mother used to hang the dozens of Christmas cards we received on those panels while the tree sat in front of the picture window for all to admire at night. The hearth had been occupied for as long as I can remember with an old pair of wooden shoes my dad had brought home from his service in Europe.

The stairs to the basement were the original sturdy planks my dad had installed so many years ago. Along the way, half the basement had been finished with walls and a tile floor, making it a hobby or sewing room.

Other than the addition of the sunroom built on the very slab I had labored over so many years ago plus the other small changes and different paint colors, the rest of the house was the same. After a few moments, I nodded my head with some reverence and sighed deeply.

"Are you thinking of moving back to Danbury?" Martha's eyebrows were raised. "Because I'm selling this house."

I stopped breathing. My mind raced. Although I wasn't ready to move north for about a year, how could I bypass the chance to buy the home in which I grew up? It was impulsive, but I couldn't shake her hand fast enough. Before I left town, we came up with a mutually agreeable number and I headed back to Florida.

We, and when I say we, I mean two real estate attorneys did the paperwork by mail and fax and Martha hooked me up with a rental agent to lease and manage the property until I was ready to make my move. It was with quiet satisfaction that I signed the extensive package of paperwork and shipped it off.

Chapter Thirty-Eight

There were a couple of banners situated between the columns of the church. One proclaimed an upcoming concert in the sanctuary and the other looked just like the magnetic sign on Herb's car – COMING SOON Lundy Life Skills. Harry led the couple down the path next to the sanctuary and into one of the buildings in the rear of the property, pointing out their office space.

"You see, Herb, the church has lost members over the years and it's an old building that needs lots of maintenance. The congregation had to come up with the money for a new boiler not long ago and a wicked blizzard damaged part of the roof. The expenses keep adding up." Harry directed Herb and June back towards the street.

"But it's still open, right?"

"Well, yes, there is still a congregation, but they're looking to make a partnership deal with the city. The congregation would get perpetual rights to worship, host weddings, and funerals, and use the church offices and music space. The city would be able to use or designate some of the other office spaces and use the sanctuary to host concerts and events. Kind of a win-win situation if you look at it that way."

The sanctuary did have superb acoustics, Herb knew that much from experience. Out by the curb, he pointed to the Lundy banner.

"What's this all about?"

"This is why you are needed in 2019, Herb. There are just too many kids that have either lost their way or never had one, to begin with. Parents are also missing a bunch of life skills you and I might take for granted. Many of our schools trend well below state proficiency averages. You and June are to run this ministry to serve some of these young people and in fact, their parents, who are identified through social workers, community aid agencies, or seek assistance on their own. They need basic training in life skills. They want a better life; they just don't know how to do it." Frankly, neither did Herb nor June know how they would provide that training.

"Harry, how are we supposed to afford all this? I mean, we don't have any kind of income; we don't really know a whole lot about helping these kids. In fact, we don't know anything about teaching life skills."

"Don't worry, Herb. It's in your heart to do it and that will get you started. And besides, you've got a grant from the city to get this thing off the ground. You can come back later to check out your office and here are the keys." Harry handed over the keys with his left hand and grabbed Herb's right hand in his own, looking him in the eye.

"You'll be fine, Herb. You too, June. I've been waiting for this for a long time. Shame to see things come to this, but you're needed. You're needed now. You won't let us down." His confidence was reassuring, and truth be told, somewhat overwhelming.

"We'll do our best. We will."

"Now, you can take me home. It's an ALF over on Kenosia Avenue. You know where that is, I'd imagine."

Kenosia Avenue was pretty darn close to the old Magic Dairy; of course, Herb knew exactly where to go.

"Harry. What's an ALF?"

Before long, the old Ford drew into the parking lot for the assisted living facility, marked "Visitor Parking Only."

"Herb, this is where old folks like me live. Some of us anyway. There are still families that care for their own but when you need some help getting by and family doesn't cut it, this is it. They feed you, make sure you take your medication, clean up after you, that sort of thing." It made sense.

"Medicare pays for that, too?"

"Well, some of it anyway. It helps to have a few dollars put away. These places aren't cheap."

"Say, what was that raised-up road we

passed under back there?"

"That's right. You left before the Interstate system got going. That's an Interstate highway, Herb. Kind of a high-speed road to get you anywhere in the country almost. Eisenhower started it. You might remember that." Herb did recall reading about it but never saw one.

"How fast can you go on the Interstate?"

"Well, most folks go about seventy or so, but I've seen 'em speed by doing eighty or ninety. State Patrol likes those. Makes a hefty speeding ticket. This one here is Interstate 84. Takes you to Hartford going that way and connects just over the state line to other Interstates in New York. Let me go. I'll be in touch." Harry fibbed. "There's a smartphone for you in the church office and an instruction book. You'll be fine." And with that, Harry was gone, hobbling into the main building entrance, waving to familiar faces as he stepped on the automatic door opener.

Herb yelled out but Harry didn't hear him. "Hey, Harry! What's an Uber?"

June, despite all the newness, crazy prices and changes, was calm but Herb was not. He had at least a thousand questions all vying for space in his frontal lobe. He didn't know where to begin, what to do, where to go. Panicky, he looked at June's pleasant smile. She was good with it. He was not. Not yet.

"Now what?" It was all Herb could muster. The only thing that made sense, the only thread holding everything together was the fact they were still in Danbury. Sixty-two years later, but still home. That would have to be enough, at least for the moment.

"Let's head back to the church." June dangled the office keys in her hand. "I bet we'll find a few answers there." Herb pursed his lips in thought for a moment, then nodded. He looked at June and nodded again.

"You're right. Let's go." With that, Herb did another three-point turn and headed back out to Kenosia Avenue turning on to Backus Avenue past some completely unfamiliar buildings and stores, passing what should have been the Danbury Fair until it became Park Avenue, running underneath that Interstate. He saw buildings with weird names like Xfinity and a Christmas Tree Shop. Why would Christmas trees need a shop? The huge shopping center, the Danbury Fair Mall seemed to go on forever and had a parking lot big enough for thousands of fairgoers. He shook his head. Greed, he thought. The money offer was one the fair trustees couldn't refuse. So sad. And to sully the name of the great fair by attaching it to a bunch of stores. No shame.

Eventually, he turned left onto Division Street, then quickly right on West Street towards the church. The roads were mostly familiar as were some of the homes but stores with strange names and more than a few unfamiliar restaurants dotted the built-up landscape. He remarked to June about the price of gas.

Along the way, Herb noted the huge variety of cars and trucks on the road, many with names he'd never seen before. He saw unfamiliar brands such as Hyundai, Lexus, Subaru, Kia, Toyota, Acura, and some familiar names too including Chevrolet, Ford, Dodge, and others. So many cars resembled puffed up and sleek station wagons. A few had the word "hybrid" in chrome script. Pickup trucks had gotten huge since the 1950s and seemed fancier than most of the cars. They all resembled the futuristic-looking vehicles predicted in Popular Mechanics and Popular Science magazines from decades ago.

He saw several cars with apparently crazy people alone inside talking aloud to no one and gesturing while they drove. There were no flying vehicles he could see, but Herb saw a kid gliding along and balancing on a two-wheeled board. People stared at his car out of curiosity and Herb stared right back.

Herb and June were indeed home, but not home at the same time. What's unfamiliar can also be scary. Herb was scared.

Chapter Thirty-Nine

Herb pulled into the church parking lot once again and shut off the motor. He pointed towards the picnic basket. "Is there any coffee?" The coffee was tepid but drinkable and June poured some out into the thermos cup. Herb sipped it while his mind raced. He took June's hand in his own. A calming feeling began to overtake his nervousness. He glanced in the rearview mirror and for a moment thought he saw the man who'd sent them here. Then just as quickly, he was gone.

"We're going to be OK," Herb finally decided. "It's going to work out. We'll do what we need to do and we're not alone." He peered up at the clock face of the church. The minute hand moved.

Herb and June took the sidewalk past the sanctuary all the way to the back buildings. A small directory indicated their office space. The old floors creaked beneath their feet but momentarily they arrived at the door Harry had pointed out with a paper note taped to it. "Lundy" is all it said. The door was locked. June took the key that looked like a door key and opened it. The space was impressive; big enough to host small group meetings, a large desk with some kind of vertical flat panel on top of it, a bookcase, and some stackable chairs near the far wall. June walked over to the desk while Herb surveyed the space.

"What do you think this is all about?" Herb wondered aloud.

"I think I know," replied June. "Here, look at this." She handed Herb a three-fold brochure with that name again, Lundy Life Skills, the address of the office, a phone number and some long run-on word – lundylifeskills -with three "w's" in front of it followed by a period and the word, "com." Inside, there was a summary of services provided by this Lundy Life Skills, only some of which Herb felt comfortable in delivering. Mentoring, Good Parenting (they weren't even parents), Career Guidance and something called Learning Life Skills.

"Have you been taking classes I don't know about?" Herb gave June a questioning look.

"Well no, but we could do these things, don't you think? I mean, if this is why we're here, to make a difference in our Danbury of the future, we must have the ability. We just need faith to do it."

Herb nodded. Why not? He felt like they were up to any task. Looking at the items on the desk, he touched a small device that looked like a potato cut in half lengthwise except it was made from plastic and had a couple of button things formed in the shape of it and a little wheel sticking out from the top. Instantly, the panel thing on the desk lit up. It displayed a message on what was a flat TV screen in color that said, "Windows 10." Whatever that was. In a couple of moments, a beautiful image of a glacier appeared, and a series of small boxes popped up in different colors and shapes. Some were tagged with unfamiliar terms like, "Firefox" and "Adobe Acrobat." Others, along the bottom edge simply had little colored shapes. Herb shrugged at June. She shuffled through the top desk drawer.

"Here," she said. "Look at this book. The title is, 'Windows 10 for Dummies.' Are you a dummy, Herb?" She giggled.

"I am when it comes to something like this. Maybe this is what Harry was talking about, the FaceBook thing and whatever eBay is." He handed the potato thing with the bright light shining underneath to June and looked for any other clues he could find.

"Here's a schedule of our classes we're supposed to hold. It says, "The City of Danbury in cooperation with Lundy Life Skills provides a new series of classes for young adults, parents, and anyone seeking advice, information or assistance on the following subjects." It went on to describe the categories Herb saw in the brochure. The calendar section showed classes starting the week after Thanksgiving!

"We've got a lot of work to do, June."
Herb was concerned, but not worried. If this was
their reason for being here in 2019, then so be it.
They had to have been chosen for a specific
purpose and not by chance.

"Here's a note from Harry." June pointed
to the flat screen.

"How did you find that?" Herb wondered.

"One of the little images on the screen
said, "Harry says click here." There was an arrow
that moved on the screen when I moved the
whatever it is, potato thing, and I pressed this
little button." It was something called a "Word"
file and it said,

Dear Herb and June;

*This is Harry and I have a message for you. Of
course, you're worried that you won't be able to do the
things that brochure says, but you're both pure of
heart, you both have the values we need to spread
around this community in these times, and I wouldn't
have sent you here if I wasn't sure you would succeed.
Now, you may be wondering how you're going to get
by, how you're going to earn money. The city is going
to fund the program expenses for you in a partnership
with Danbury Youth Services, although you'll be
serving youths as well as their parents. But after you
read this, open the bottom drawer and take out the
manila envelope for your answer. I won't be seeing
you again, but remember, I am, and I love you.*

Herb wasn't sure what to make of the message. Was that Harry who rode with them in the parade? Or was it ...? What about the ALF place? And what's an Uber? Was Harry someone else? Was he maybe the Holy Spirit in a form to which they could relate? What about the Trinity? Who was the man he met in the park and who sent them here? Was he the same as Harry?

These questions slightly troubled but did not worry Herb because by now he had long learned to trust what was put on his heart. He knew full well that some things simply required faith and had no explanation that he could comprehend. The endless card catalog, the ability to move through time, a parallel existence even. June pulled the envelope from the bottom drawer, just as the note described. Herb opened it and pulled out something that looked very formal; a lease agreement of some sort.

"This says we have a lease for one year on a home on Seeley Street." He read further. It's a Cape Cod-style home, three bedrooms, two baths. I think I know this home." In fact, there was a photograph of it attached to the final page of the agreement. "Yeah, that's the one, but it's been updated a bit. I started delivering there right after it was built. Well, sixty-two years ago. Huh." There was a letter attached.

"Here, it says the owner bought the place last year but isn't ready to move in, so it was made available to rent. Guy's moving from Florida about a year from now."

So, they had a place to live. There were two house keys rattling around inside as well along with something called an access code for an alarm system. Why would a house need an alarm? Putting that thought aside, Herb pulled out another item from the envelope. It was a textured piece of heavy paper with some embossed or raised lettering.

"What is it?" June was anxious to know.

"Well, it's got our names on it. Looks official. Best I can tell, it's a stock certificate for one thousand shares of something called Amazon dot com." June was intrigued but just shrugged. Putting it down, Herb said, "We'll have to check that out."

###

Epilogue

Herb and June worked overtime for the first month and a half, getting ready to host their initial class, Career Guidance. Thinking there had to be a major common-sense component, it was something to which they could relate, and to which they could certainly bring a unique perspective from a simpler time. Herb took a crash course (online) in conversational Spanish and did well enough to greet his Hispanic participants in their preferred language. Over time, he would master it and become known as a trusted friend of the immigrant community.

June focused on learning how to use the computer and the equally powerful smartphone. In less than a week, she was clicking and typing and doing Google searches like it was as natural as knitting a sweater. Soon, she was preparing lesson handouts for the Career Guidance class. The little flat keyboard was so much easier to use than the Royal typewriter with which she was familiar. The best thing was being able to correct typing errors without having to use "Mistake-Out." Most of the careers she found were completely foreign to her but in the end, whether it was for a database analyst, a phlebotomist, or even an Uber driver (they finally figured that one out) it was not so much the job or the skills required, as much as how to present oneself, be truthful, sincere, follow through on any interview, and to be polite and energetic. These were attributes that were a given in 1957 but somehow had fallen into disrepair over the last six decades. June learned quickly how to craft a great resumé and cover letter and helped her students with play-acting interviews, a key factor in obtaining employment. Lundy Life Skills quickly became known as the place to go in Danbury if you wanted help to find a good job.

As they moved into the new year, the Lundy's learned all about the best ways to serve as mentors and matched volunteers from the now growing church congregation and elsewhere to those in need, serving as mentor-finders and interacting on a need basis. Good Parenting classes came later. On a fast track, the state certified June and Herb to be licensed foster parents and they welcomed three siblings into their home on Seeley Street, the two boys in the bedroom to the right on the second floor and the older girl in the other bedroom, all to herself.

After learning with great joy and no small surprise that their stock shares of Amazon were worth a truly hefty sum, Herb and June redeemed enough to open a trust that would provide a monthly income and help fund a substantial program for residents on Learning

Life Skills. Very shortly, the Learning Life Skills class turned out to be the most important and valuable outreach of them all and Herb and June quickly realized that this was the real reason they'd been chosen to come to 2019 and share the wisdom and genuineness of times gone by.

A curriculum quickly developed as the Lundy's applied everyday principles of the late 1950s to the world of 2019 starting with things like personal accountability, how to open and maintain a bank account, the right way to apply for a job and how to follow up, successful study habits for school and beyond, communication including writing proficiency, teamwork, public speaking, critical thinking and problem solving.

These were needed skills mysteriously and virtually absent from any other syllabus available and with the number of single-parent households or where parents had to work two jobs to get by, neither were these skills learned at home. Herb and June brought a conviction and confidence and fiery enthusiasm to their Life Skills presentations that some said were reminiscent of the late Doctor Billy Graham.

The six-week course also included the importance of paying attention to detail and as June discovered, identified the need for and inclusion of advanced data analysis skills. Often learning as they went, Herb and June were usually just one step ahead of those they were teaching. Once developed, the course attracted maxed-out sessions and even the city sent employees to take advantage of the desperately needed skills. Eventually, the mayor's office asked if Herb and June could participate in something called a webinar to share the success of their program with the governor's office.

Intertwined in these needed skills and assimilated into the presentation were woven the aspects of love, joy, and peace; patience, kindness, and goodness; faithfulness, gentleness, and self-control. They were evident in the sincerity with which each lesson was taught; in the genuine concern the Lundy's had for the wellbeing and progress of their students. There could be no argument against these virtues and just as they had been when written two-thousand years ago, rang true in the dangerous and complicated world of 2019. June and Herb led the classes in a tag-team format and gently but emphatically imbued every practical skill with humanity and humility. After much practice and role-playing with June, Herb introduced the first session of each class with a passion that was unmistakably genuine.

"I'd like to welcome you to our Learning Life Skills class and invite you to stop me at any point if you have a question or comment." He scanned the room. "OK? So, what can we learn over the next six weeks from the actions and behaviors that were important to our parents and grandparents?

Someone called out, "Don't get old!" The group laughed.

"Excellent point, but I can tell you that age can and frequently does yield wisdom (looking over at June and winking) and we should probably take advantage of the knowledge gained and trusted over the decades. Make sense?" Most everyone nodded in agreement.

"Alright. Now in this course, we want you to learn and assimilate some basic life skills that you may have missed along the way that will truly make your life fuller, more affordable, and easier to navigate. For example; how many of you have a checking account?" About two-thirds of the group raised hands. "How many of you know the overdraft fee your bank will charge if you bounce a check?" No hands. "How many of you know how to avoid being charged an overdraft fee?" No hands.

"If you write a check or send a payment that cannot be covered by your balance, the bank may pay it but charge you thirty-five dollars or more." Murmuring from the class. "Not only that, if you have three payments that are in overdraft status, you'll pay three times thirty-five dollars. How many of you can afford that?" No hands were raised. "We're going to show you the importance and methods of managing your checking balance and a smart way to avoid ever having to pay an overdraft fee. Sound good?" A few "yes" comments and heads nodding. "OK then. Let's get started."

Later in the year, the lease on the Seeley Street house ended and it was time to move. A three-bedroom cottage on Mountainville Road past the point where it split off to Southern Boulevard came available and with their finances secured, the Lundy's bought it and moved with their three foster children who were now being considered for adoption. Smart Parenting, indeed. June found that she could have written the program materials all by herself after dealing with three energetic young ones.

The flight to Bradley was a typical Southwest Airlines trip; a goofy cabin steward, enough legroom even for my six-foot-two frame, and a can of sparkling water. The route from Hartford to Danbury was easily remembered and I steered the rental Ford Escape to exit the highway at Newtown Road, taking roads that were still etched into my brain. I wasn't quite ready to move but came up to take possession of the home since the lease was expiring. The interactive map feature on the seven-inch screen reminded me where to turn but I didn't really need it. I met the leasing agent and the occupants at the Union Savings Bank on Main Street near Elmwood Park to do some paperwork and secure the house keys. Coffee was brought in.

Herb stood and spoke; "Mr. Holmes, a pleasure. This is my wife, June." I returned their warm smiles. There was something special about these two. It was obvious. The serenity about them; a kind of warm confidence. I immediately felt an unmistakable kinship.

"The pleasure is all mine, I assure you."

I told them the history of the home, how it was constructed and by whom. I shared tales of growing up on Seeley Street, and they relayed some of the details of their life skills operation at my old church.

Saying our goodbyes at the bank, the Lundy's headed back to the church office and I drove directly to my home, my old and my new home on Seeley Street. Along the way I considered setting up my work desk and computer at the bay window so my imagination could fly like the snow flurries on the twisting wind. They say you can't go home again, but to my mind, it was worth a try. I contemplated ordering Charles Chips from Amazon and getting milk and eggs delivered from Stew Leonard's. Things change of course but maybe not as much as we think.

Thinking about the little voids my dad built into the upstairs bedrooms, I wondered if I might find an old box of baseball cards in one of those secret spaces. I spied my grandparents' old house on the curve where Grand Street begins as I turned left on Mountainville then right on Seeley. Driving purposely and slowly as the hill gathered its upward slope, I eased the rental car into the driveway and walked that same old sidewalk to the front door. On the top step there sat a vintage galvanized box. The faded lettering read, "Magic Dairy."

An old Danbury friend Marc Catone and his sister Sara on the front step of their Putnam Drive home with a fictional Magic Dairy milk box, circa 1960.
(Modified photo courtesy of Marc Catone, used with permission)

Before You Go

Please consider donating to Americares for disaster relief. Americares has been serving the world since 1975 and by design, has an impressive efficiency rate of around 97% meaning, just 3% of your donation is used to pay for overhead and staff. The remainder directly aids those in need here in the United States, throughout the Caribbean and the Americas, and elsewhere.

Americares obtains donated goods, supplies, and medicines from corporations with whom they have established long-standing relationships. Your donation helps them pay for the logistics required to move these acutely needed supplies around the world, putting them directly into the hands of those in need, avoiding any potential mishandling issues. In my opinion, Roberto Clemente would have been well pleased with Americares and it is my wish that you seek more information online at www.americares.org.

Thank you!

About the Author

Mark T. Holmes is an author, commercial writer, and former marketing executive. Following a layoff from a lucrative senior marketing job at one of the nation's largest credit unions in 2009, Mr. Holmes formed his own Florida S-corporation, Idea Depot, Inc., and began writing high-end military transition and executive federal resumes, along with doing web development and optimization work, plus marketing writing for a national message-on-hold company.

In 2014, Mr. Holmes released his first book, *Streams to Ford*, a book of poetry long in the making, followed in 2015 by *Always Ready – Coast Guard Sea Stories from the 1970s*. In 2016, he released *Artifact* – a World War II spy novel based on his father's missions as a B-24 bomber pilot. All books are available in print and Kindle format on Amazon.

Mark and his wife Sheri operate a retail location in an antique mall, and trade in antiques and vintage cameras.

Learn more, read FAQ, and see additional commentary online at:
http://www.herblundybook.com

On FaceBook (like my page) at:
https://www.facebook.com/HerbLundyandtheMagicMilkTruck/

Here are links to my other publications:

http://www.artifactbook.com – World War 2 spy novel inspired by my dad's missions as a B-24 pilot.

http://www.alwaysreadybook.com – Coast Guard Sea Stories from the 1970s, an anthology of my time in the service, 1971 to 1979 with stories woven together by songs of the '70s.

https://www.facebook.com/StreamsToFord/ Awkward poetry, if you're really hard up for something to read.

On Kindle only, *The Last Flight of Chauncey Freeman*, a short story about a genuine WW2 hero from Texas who gave all for his country and the story of his fellow crew member, told in a Paul Harvey style: **https://amzn.to/2q1rX1w**

Made in the USA
Middletown, DE
19 September 2023

38809755R00155